"Just get out of

He got out, closed t
steps. But he stalled.
he had to do. He rounded the hood and opened up the driver's side door.

Jane glared up at him. "What?"

"Get out of the car."

She didn't argue, but got out. She folded her arms over her chest and lifted her chin defiantly.

If he took a second to think about it, he would have probably realized what a stupid move this was.

But he didn't think about it. He dropped his bag and kissed her.

Kissed her long and deep.

She leaned into him and his body reacted.

How long had it been since he'd kissed anyone like this?

He didn't know…didn't care.

She tasted warm and soft…sweet. Just like he'd known she would.

His arms went around her, pulling her closer, tucking her hips against his. She made the sweetest sound.

But he had to go.…

Dear Reader,

Thank you so much for choosing my book. This story represents a major milestone for me. *His Secret Life* is the thirty-fourth COLBY AGENCY story. I am so proud to be a part of the Harlequin Intrigue family. I hope you will enjoy this latest installment, the third in the ELITE RECONNAISSANCE DIVISION trilogy.

This year marks a couple more very important milestones as well. For one, this is Harlequin Intrigue's 25th anniversary. Imagine, for twenty-five years Harlequin Intrigue has been bringing readers a breath-stealing ride with suspense, thrills and, of course, romance. Readers never have to wonder what they'll get when they pick up an Intrigue. From the high-octane action, the gut-wrenching suspense, the most wicked villain to the sweet and sizzling connection between the hero and heroine, Intrigue always delivers as promised. Harlequin Intrigue is a fast and furious read each and every month!

Also, this year is Harlequin's 60th anniversary! No other publisher has consistently brought romance to readers in every possible setting and with every imaginable scenario the way Harlequin has. Whether a small-town girl racing toward her future with an international tycoon or a sexy billionairess seeking refuge in the arms of a big strong cowboy far away from her metropolitan home, Harlequin has it covered. Every book, every month features a new and interesting twist on the tried and true as well as in cutting-edge, previously uncharted territory. Escape, that's what Harlequin has given readers for more than half a century.

So, turn the page and escape with me!

Best,

Debra Webb

DEBRA WEBB

HIS SECRET LIFE

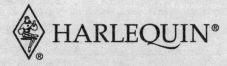

TORONTO • NEW YORK • LONDON
AMSTERDAM • PARIS • SYDNEY • HAMBURG
STOCKHOLM • ATHENS • TOKYO • MILAN • MADRID
PRAGUE • WARSAW • BUDAPEST • AUCKLAND

Recycling programs for this product may not exist in your area.

ISBN-13: 978-0-373-69424-2

HIS SECRET LIFE

This edition published by arrangement with Harlequin Books S.A.

® and TM are trademarks of the publisher. Trademarks indicated with ® are registered in the United States Patent and Trademark Office, the Canadian Trade Marks Office and in other countries.

www.eHarlequin.com

Printed in U.S.A.

ABOUT THE AUTHOR

Debra Webb was born in Scottsboro, Alabama, to parents who taught her that anything is possible if you want it bad enough. She began writing at age nine. Eventually, she met and married the man of her dreams, and tried some other occupations, including selling vacuum cleaners, working in a factory, a daycare center, a hospital and a department store. When her husband joined the military, they moved to Berlin, Germany, and Debra became a secretary in the commanding general's office. By 1985 they were back in the States, and finally moved to Tennessee, to a small town where everyone knows everyone else. With the support of her husband and two beautiful daughters, Debra took up writing again, looking to mysteries and movies for inspiration. In 1998, her dream of writing for Harlequin Books came true. You can write to Debra with your comments at P.O. Box 64, Huntland, Tennessee 37345, or visit her Web site at www.debrawebb.com to find out exciting news about her next book.

Books by Debra Webb

HARLEQUIN INTRIGUE
891—PERSON OF INTEREST
909—INVESTIGATING 101*
916—RAW TALENT*
934—THE HIDDEN HEIR*
951—A COLBY CHRISTMAS*
983—A SOLDIER'S OATH†
989—HOSTAGE SITUATION†
995—COLBY VS. COLBY†
1023—COLBY REBUILT*
1042—GUARDIAN ANGEL*
1071—IDENTITY UNKNOWN*
1092—MOTIVE: SECRET BABY
1108—SECRETS IN FOUR CORNERS
1145—SMALL-TOWN SECRETS††
1151—THE BRIDE'S SECRETS††
1157—HIS SECRET LIFE††

*Colby Agency
†The Equalizers
††Colby Agency: Elite Reconnaissance Division

CAST OF CHARACTERS

Jane Sutton—A Colby Agency investigator. Jane is looking for a hero, but does she find one?

Troy Benson—He isn't who he says he is. But is he a hero?

Bernard Beckman—He wants Troy Benson found and taken care of—permanently.

Merrilee Walters—The newest member of the Colby Agency staff.

Ian Michaels—Second in command at the Colby Agency.

Victoria Colby-Camp—The head of the Colby Agency.

Lucas Camp—Victoria's husband, a man of mystery.

Jamie Colby—Victoria's granddaughter.

Jim Colby—Victoria's only son.

Clayton Barker—The man behind the plot to kidnap Jamie Colby.

Chapter One

Victoria Colby-Camp collected her purse and prepared to order the car. Picking up her grand-daughter at school would definitely be the highlight of this day.

After spending a good portion of the morning at the E.R. with J.T. and Eve, then dealing with that unnerving call from the bastard behind the abduction attempts, Victoria had long passed exhaustion.

She needed Lucas at her side. The government contact that served as a liaison whenever Lucas was on assignment had been unable to reach him or any member of his team. The reason, of course, was classified. Victoria had put off reaching out to Lucas again as long as she dared.

She could no longer presume the threat to her

granddaughter was minimal. With that call, the danger had escalated to a new level.

This threat was not linked to Lucas or one of his personal enemies. The past had come back to haunt the Colby Agency once more.

An associate of Errol Leberman, the archnemesis of the Colby name, was behind the threat. Victoria had not recognized the caller's voice. He had refused to give his name, pushing Victoria into a corner and limiting her options to the single one she had hoped to avoid. Reaching out to Jim.

The past few years her son had taken great strides in settling into a normal, happy life. Jim and his wife, Tasha, were immensely happy and their daughter, Jamie, thrived. This extended vacation to the remotest regions of Africa was the couple's first getaway. Victoria had not wanted to disturb their escape. Her son so deserved to take a real vacation for the first time in his life. To experience an adventure that was for pure enjoyment and not related to his work.

But the caller and the situation had left Victoria no choice.

As she'd been forced to reach out to Lucas, her people had been attempting to reach Jim all day.

Recent political unrest had concerned Victoria as to their selection of this safari for their getaway. Tasha had great empathy for the country and its many woes. She had chosen the place for that reason. Jim had agreed. Victoria had reminded herself that her son was more than capable of taking care of himself and his wife in any situation. There had been no need to worry.

But that had been before. Before rumors surfaced that Jamie Colby was a target. Before they had been ambushed and three people had lost their lives.

Before the call.

Victoria shuddered as memories of Leberman and the horrors he had used against the Colby name crowded into her thoughts. Anyone associated with him would be every bit as evil and twisted. Worse, they would go to any lengths to accomplish their mission.

The possibility of their success terrified Victoria.

She swallowed back the emotions that constricted her throat. Victoria never allowed anyone or anything to shake her confidence and determination to this degree.

But this absolutely shook her to the core.

Perhaps she was not as strong as she once was.

Her office door opened, snapping her to attention.

"We have Jim on the line," Ian Michaels announced.

Simon Ruhl came in behind him, closed the door.

A mixture of relief and anticipation seared Victoria's senses. "Finally."

They moved to the conference table, where Ian activated the conferencing system. "Jim, Simon and I are in Victoria's office. Are you in a position to speak at length?"

"For as long as the connection lasts," Jim granted.

Emotion surged upon hearing her son's voice. Victoria smiled even as tears welled in her eyes. "Jim, it's good to hear your voice."

"What's wrong? I can hear the worry in *your* voice, Victoria."

Victoria had hoped at some point her son would feel comfortable calling her mother. But that hadn't happened yet. Years of brainwashing and bitterness had made any sort of intimacy on a normal level difficult. Still, their relationship was close, solid.

"There's a situation," she explained, annoyed that her voice quavered. "We had hoped to contain the threat without interfering with your vacation, but that has changed now."

"Tell me," Jim commanded, his tone fierce, "that my daughter is safe."

"Jamie is safe," Victoria hastened to assure him. "She is unharmed and having a grand time being the center of attention. We have the maximum security measures in place. For now, all is under control where her welfare is concerned."

"There's been a threat against her," Jim surmised.

His voice had lost all inflection. When threatened he closed out all emotions, a tactic he'd learned after years of abuse. Agony twisted in Victoria. She would give most anything not to have to do this to him.

"Yes," she confirmed. "Ian is going to bring you up to speed."

Surprised, Ian shifted his attention to her and Victoria nodded for him to take the reins. She did not trust herself to maintain her composure.

She looked away as Ian launched into the details of the threat to her granddaughter. More of those stinging emotions burned in her eyes. Inside, where no one could see, she trembled.

For the first time in a very long while she was afraid. Uncertain of herself. The past year her agency had worked hard to pull together a reconnaissance division specifically for finding the missing. How could her agency possess such talent and still be vulnerable to this kind of threat?

The answer was all too clear.

Leberman, an evil man with extensive power, had reached out from the grave and done this to her family. The years of torment...the struggle to overcome the misery he'd elicited in her life even now sent dread welling inside her.

The bastard.

"Victoria."

She blinked, returned her focus to the two men seated at the conference table with her. "Yes?" She mentally scrambled to catch up. Had Ian asked her a question? What had she missed?

"Jim is ready to listen to the recording."

She nodded. "Of course."

Ian gave Simon a nod. Simon initiated the playback of the recorded call.

Victoria clasped her hands in her lap, held on tightly as the sinister voice filled the room. Ten million dollars was the price for calling off the abduction of Victoria's granddaughter. But she knew that no amount of money would guarantee Jamie Colby's safety. The threat had to be neutralized at its core.

When the recording had reached an end, the silence thickened for several moments before Jim spoke.

"His name is Clayton Barker. He operated the mercenary camp where I stayed for two years. Do not underestimate him. If he's behind this…"

Victoria heard talking in the background. One voice sounded like Tasha's.

"Jim?" A new kind of tension quivered through

Victoria. The background conversation sounded clipped, tense.

"Look," Jim said, apparently moving away from the conversation in the background since the voices faded. "I'm coming home. I don't know how long it will take. There's been some trouble here."

More of that paralyzing fear streamed through Victoria's veins. "Related to the recent shift in the political climate?"

"Yes," Jim confirmed. "We thought we were safe but trouble has moved into this area. We were already preparing to move out before your call was patched through. Tasha and I will head back to Kenya and get on the first flight back home."

"Can we get a helicopter to your location to facilitate your departure?" Ian suggested.

"Won't work. The government has shut down all air traffic in the area. We'll have to try getting out in the jeeps. If that doesn't work, we'll do it on foot. I will get there, one way or another."

"Jim." Victoria worked at keeping her voice even. "Are you and Tasha safe for now?"

"For now." His tone was grave.

Adrenaline fired through Victoria and she snatched back her crumbling resolve and courage. "Listen to me, Jim," she said, her voice stronger than before, "you take care of yourself and your wife. Make your way back here, but don't take unnecessary risks. All of us are working on this situation. We will find Barker and we will do whatever necessary to stop him. Jamie will be protected. Do not doubt that for a moment. You have my word."

Her resolve buckled for a minute, but there was no way Victoria Colby-Camp was going to be undone by a degenerate like Barker. She would prevail. She looked from Ian to Simon. She had the best of the best behind her.

"I know you'll do all you can," Jim said, "but I can't risk that it might not be enough. I'm coming back. Nothing here will stop me."

The call ended with one last plea from Victoria for him to take care.

He needn't worry, she would not let him down. Not again.

As much as she understood that her son loved her and that his words were not a reflection of her failure, she knew what his statement meant.

Victoria had done all within her power to keep Jim safe as a child.

And it hadn't been enough.

Chapter Two

At 4:20 p.m. Victoria's final appointment for the day arrived. Stuart Norcross settled into a chair flanking her desk. ·

"I know we just spoke on Friday," he began, "but I'm anxious to see how your investigation is going."

Victoria picked up the file Mildred had placed on her desk. "Completely understandable, Stuart." She smiled. "Your wife and son are safe thanks to this man and you'd like to be able to properly show your gratitude."

"Precisely." Stuart settled back into his chair, the tension in his regal frame receding marginally.

Stuart Norcross was one of Chicago's leading entrepreneurs. Despite the struggling economy, Stuart had taken his custom personal chef service nationwide. Having devoted most of his life to building his business, he had only in the past few years taken time for a true personal life. He'd met and married a wonderful woman and they'd had their first child just two years ago.

Victoria checked her notes. "His name is Troy Benson. Jane Sutton, one of our investigators specifically trained for finding the missing, has located Mr. Benson and is preparing for contact. I expect to have feedback no later than tomorrow afternoon."

"Outstanding." Stuart smiled, his relief palpable. "I knew I could depend on your agency, Victoria."

"Thank you, Stuart. We pride ourselves on thorough, efficient work."

Stuart inclined his head and studied her a moment. "Do you have any idea as to why Mr. Benson left the scene so suddenly?"

One week ago Stuart's wife, Reese, had visited an old friend in Meriden. Driving back to Chicago late that evening in the pouring rain, their son asleep in his car seat, Reese had braked hard to avoid a dog and lost control of the vehicle. The car had plunged off the road and into a dangerously deep ravine. Thankfully a thicket of small trees had stopped the vehicle before it crashed headlong into the rocks below. Badly injured, Reese had realized that the protection of the trees wouldn't last but there was nothing she could do. The sound of splintering wood and straining metal had warned that if she and the baby didn't get out of the car in a hurry, they would surely plunge to the bottom any second.

Seemingly out of nowhere, a man appeared. He rescued the baby from his car seat and barely got Reese out of the driver's seat before the car broke through the trees and pitched to the bottom of the ravine. After checking their injuries and calling for help, the man disappeared during the chaos of the police and rescue personnel's arrival on the scene.

"Not just yet," Victoria explained. "We believe the man is using an alias." At Stuart's surprised look, she added, "There could be any number of reasons that have nothing to do with criminal activity. A former celebrity." She flared her hands. "A recluse for purely personal reasons. That's why we're going to take a cautious approach from this point forward. Though I understand that you're very grateful for what Mr. Benson did, it would be in your best interest to know who this man is and what his motives for seclusion are before moving forward with a meeting between the two of you."

Stuart nodded. "I suppose you're right. I certainly don't want to endanger my family by becoming involved with a man with a troubled past."

"Unfortunately," Victoria offered, "it goes with the territory, Stuart." She knew this all too well.

"Wealth and power can sometimes prove a magnet for those seeking easy money. Self-protection is essential. If we uncover disturbing details perhaps it would be wisest to show your gratitude anonymously through my investigator."

"So his name is definitely not Troy Benson? How did you find him?"

"My investigator, Jane, used the description your wife gave of the man who rescued her to start the search. Since the man was thought to be on foot that night, our first assumption would be that he lived nearby. Along that deserted stretch of road, there are only a few scattered communities. The occasional farm, but not much else. We focused on anything within walking distance."

"Reese vividly recalls catching a glimpse of someone as her car spun out of control," Stuart confirmed. "She believes he was, indeed, on foot."

"That being the case," Victoria went on, "we assumed that the man was likely from somewhere nearby. Jane checked the surrounding communities until she found someone matching the description. He goes by the name Troy Benson and he works at a diner in Plano."

"If your investigator hasn't spoken to this man yet, how can she be sure it's him—other than the description my wife gave, I mean? This Troy Benson could simply be someone who looks like the man who rescued my family. Is she sure it's him?"

Again, Stuart's anxiousness was showing. He wanted this man found, but he also wanted to find the hero he had created in his mind. "Reese stated that the man who rescued her cut his left forearm as he pulled her from the damaged car, correct?"

Stuart sat forward a little. "Yes. Yes, she did. Does this Troy Benson have an injury consistent with what my wife recalls?"

"He does. Jane has him under surveillance and is hoping for an opportunity to lift a latent print. We can have a friend at the bureau, as well as our Chicago PD liaison, run the print through the systems to see if he shows up in any databases."

"You'll keep me informed?" Stuart asked, his expression clearly crestfallen.

"Absolutely."

Victoria's client stood, sighed. "The waiting game it is, then."

"It won't be long," Victoria assured him. "Trust me, Stuart, Jane will work as quickly as possible."

When Stuart had taken his leave, Victoria stood for a long moment staring at the door that separated her office from the small private lobby where Mildred greeted clients and took care of Victoria's calendar.

Waiting was the hardest thing to do.

A person's whole life was spent waiting on one thing or another. For Christmas to arrive. To find love. For the safe birth of a child...to live without fear.

Waiting was all Victoria could do for now as well.

Chapter Three

Plano, Illinois, 4:30 p.m.

The Sunshine Diner was filled to capacity as usual. Jane selected the only vacant stool at the counter to facilitate a better view of the kitchen's serving window.

An apron-clad Troy Benson set two plates on the serving window ledge and announced, "Order up."

With his shirtsleeves pushed up, the bandage on his left arm was visible.

"You ready to order?"

Jane dragged her attention from the window to the waitress who'd stopped on the other side of the counter. "I'll have the special." Burger and fries. A girl couldn't go wrong with the basics.

The waitress, Patsy, scratched the order on her

pad, flashed a smile and headed over to post the order on the cook's wheel in the service window.

Benson glanced at Jane as he tugged her order from the wheel. Jane held his gaze, wanting him to know she wasn't here for the food. She'd come in and out the past couple of days. She felt certain he realized she was watching him, but he hadn't gotten nervous just yet.

She'd been cautious with her questioning of the locals. Not wanting to spook him, she'd resisted talking to the waitresses or the busboy in the diner.

Benson drove a beat-up old truck. The license plate was registered to a Troy Benson, originally from Michigan. His driver's license went back four years. No work or credit record for six years prior to that. Mainly because the man, the real Troy Benson, with that Social Security number had some nine years ago entered a private extended-care facility in Michigan after a tragic automobile accident. Since the facility wasn't funded by government insurance, there was no reason for any government agency to be suspicious of the use of the Social Security number some five years later. While the real Troy Benson withered away in Michigan, this pretender had started a whole new life in Illinois.

If Jane could get this guy's prints, it would be reasonably easy to determine if he had a criminal record or if perhaps he was in Witness Protection. There had to be a motive for his having taken an alias and living such a low-profile life. A low-profile life, according to the few people she'd questioned, that he went to great extents to keep very personal.

After work Benson drove his ancient truck to an equally aged farmhouse on Grissom Spring Road. He had no friends, no social life that anyone she'd asked was aware of. He had simply blown into town, driving that old truck, four years ago and had been working at the diner since.

He didn't look like a short-order cook.

Tall, well-muscled, mid-thirties, blond hair, blue eyes. Damned good looking. A little glimmer of warmth swirled beneath her belly button. Any woman would have to be in a coma or dead not to notice how handsome he was. But guys who looked like that never took a second look at Jane.

Plain Jane.

Her nickname in grade school had followed her into adulthood. She hadn't bothered attempting to dispel the unflattering moniker. She liked wearing jeans and T-shirts when she was off duty. Even on duty she stuck with serviceable slacks and conservative blouses along with practical shoes. And she hated makeup and all the hair fuss that most women took great pride in skillfully sporting.

If that, along with her generic brown hair and eyes, made her a plain Jane, then so be it.

"Here ya go."

Patsy settled a stoneware plate in front of Jane. "Thanks." Jane considered the burger and fries. "How about some coleslaw?" What she needed was a small enough item touched by the cook that she could take with her. And return it, of course, once she'd lifted the necessary prints. She'd noticed some side orders, coleslaw in particular, were served in bowls small enough to suit her requirement.

"Sure thing." Patsy strolled back to the window. "Need an order of coleslaw, Troy."

Benson flicked another of those suspicious glances from the waitress to Jane. Troy disappeared from the window for a moment and returned with a small, single-serving-size stoneware bowl of slaw. Patsy immediately placed the side order in front of Jane.

"Great." Careful not to touch the little bowl with her fingers, she dug in. She was starved. Though she'd been in the diner earlier this afternoon, she hadn't ordered anything but coffee until now. As she ate, she covertly kept an eye on Benson. The waitresses were hustling to refill drinks and take orders since the evening crowd was slowly drifting into the diner.

The bustle of the kitchen staff was also obvious beyond the serving window. While the waitresses were preoccupied with their evening rush, Jane pulled a couple of plastic sandwich bags from her purse and picked up the bowl, using one of the bags as a barrier between her fingers and the stoneware. With her movements hidden beneath the counter now, she slipped the empty bowl into the second bag and tucked it into her purse.

With a quick check to ensure that no one was paying attention, she grabbed the side order bowl left by the customer who'd abandoned the stool next to her and placed it by her plate. No need to call attention to the fact that she'd taken the bowl.

Patsy strolled past, slowing long enough to refill Jane's soda.

Her phone vibrated. With another perusal around the diner, Jane reached into the pocket of her pants and pulled out her phone to check the screen. Text message from Ian Michaels. Rendezvous with MW 5:00?

Jane responded with a suggestion of five-fifteen. OK flashed on the screen. The newest member of the Colby Agency's staff, Merrilee Walters, would come by the Plano Hotel at five-fifteen to pick up whatever Jane had been able to retrieve that might provide Benson's prints.

Excellent timing. Evidently she'd already been in the area since the office in Chicago was more than an hour away. That a member of the agency staff was standing by, indicated that the client was getting anxious. He wanted the name of the hero who'd rescued his wife and son.

Jane polished off her burger, paid her check, left a generous tip and headed for the rendezvous with Merri. The hotel was only a few blocks from the diner, so Jane had chosen to walk. According to one of the waitresses, the entire diner staff worked until around eight cleaning up and prepping for the next day. Benson wasn't likely going anywhere before eight.

And if he did, Jane knew where he lived. She was waiting for one thing, approval to approach. That approval would come when the Colby Agency had done all possible to rule out a criminal record.

As Jane rounded the corner at the end of the block, she hesitated. The sun hovered above the trees, still generating enough heat to draw a sweat. The occasional car rolled down the street. A few pedestrians were out and about. Still, that creepy sensation that crawls up the back of one's neck had camped at the base of her skull.

Jane stopped, turned around.

Nothing.

Her instincts still humming, Jane sped up her pace and made it to the hotel in record time. She surveyed the block in both directions. Nothing or no one appeared out of place. No sign of Merri.

Jane waited out front until her colleague arrived. She parked at the curb and Jane slid into the passenger seat, thankful for the cold air blasting from the air-conditioning vents.

"Any trouble finding the place?" Jane was careful to wait until Merri had turned in her direction before speaking. The newest member of the Colby Agency staff was deaf. She was inordinately skilled at lip-reading.

"Your directions were very clear." Merri glanced around the street. "Has your target noticed your presence yet?"

"He's suspicious." Jane couldn't help wishing she'd been born with Merri's bright blue eyes and silky blond hair. Truth was, no one was really ever happy with their appearance. At least that was what she told herself each time she had a "plain" moment. "I think he's keeping an eye on me."

"I guess I should make this quick, then," Merri suggested. "I don't want to draw any unnecessary attention."

She was right. Jane retrieved the bagged side order bowl and passed it to her colleague. "The waitress may have blurred Benson's prints, but it was the best I could do for now."

Merri placed the bag in the console of her sedan. "I'll get this to Ian this evening. He has a friend from CPD and one from the bureau standing by."

"Good. Maybe we'll know something early tomorrow morning."

"That's Ian's goal."

Before getting out, Jane hesitated. "How's Victoria?" The last couple of weeks had taken a tremendous toll on the head of the Colby Agency. Her granddaughter's safety was at stake and the source of the threat was still untraceable. Victoria now knew his identity, but finding him was proving impossible.

Merri's expression turned grim. "She's holding up." She shook her head. "The little girl, she doesn't really understand what's going on. Which is good."

Until now Jane hadn't noticed the slight distortion in Merri's speech. Maybe because they hadn't talked alone like this before. Merri had been deaf for about six years now. Her speech had begun to suffer in the extended period without the resonance of sound to maintain rhythm and modulation.

"Have a safe trip back to the city."

Merri nodded. "Ian will be in touch."

Jane watched Merri drive away. After living her entire life in the South, Merri was certainly getting her bearings in what she teasingly called Yankee territory.

Fishing for her keys in her purse, Jane walked toward the car she'd rented for this assignment. By the time she drove back to the diner, the dinner crowd would have thickened. Taking up a surveillance post nearby would be fairly simple.

She wasn't cleared to approach Benson yet, but keeping an eye on him in case he decided to cut and run was essential. Norcross was insistent on learning as much information as possible on Benson.

She slid behind the wheel and drove the few blocks to the diner. Parking down the block and on the other side of the street, she watched the customers filter in and out. Even with the windows down, the July heat was sweltering.

From time to time she got out and walked a short distance, just to stretch her legs and get some air flowing beneath her blouse.

More than two hours passed before the waitresses started to, one by one, head out the front entrance. The brightly colored neon sign that announced the diner was open for business went dark. Benson came out the back door a couple of times pulling a trash container. Another employee hustled out to help him dump the containers. The second time, Benson paused before going back inside. He surveyed the street, his gaze settling on Jane's car.

Oh yeah, he was well aware that he was being watched.

If he had something to hide, he might very well ditch his comfy life.

Jane watched him swagger back to the rear entrance. His suspicious glances piqued her curiosity. "What are you hiding, Mr. Benson?"

Pretty soon the lights went out inside the establishment and the kitchen staff trickled out the rear entrance. Benson waved good-night to his coworkers and headed for his old blue truck. He climbed inside and backed out of his parking slot. He hesitated at the street, probably checking out her position again before driving away.

Jane gave him a few seconds' head start before executing a U-turn and following. He'd already made the turn that led deep into the woods when she reached the turnoff to Grissom Spring Road. His farmhouse sat a couple of miles into the woods. At one time the farm had been pastureland and cultivated acreage, but for the past fifteen or so years the woods had closed in, leaving a small yard around the old house.

There were no streetlights on the old road, making the path dark beneath the canopy of ancient trees. Jane's weapon was in the rental car's console. But before she got out of the car, it would be in her purse. She was no fool. Being armed, especially on an assignment like this, was the only way to go.

She passed Benson's place and almost braked, but checked the urge at the last moment. His truck wasn't in the driveway.

What the hell?

When she'd rolled past his property far enough to be unseen, she braked to a stop and shoved the gearshift into Park. How had she lost him? There were only a couple of turns between town and his place, other than driveways leading to residences and those were few and far between.

"Damn it."

She reached for the gearshift. *Turn around and pick a spot to wait him out.* If he didn't show up in a reasonable length of time, she'd have no choice but to hunt him down.

"Get out of the car."

Jane's breath caught at the shouted command. She turned to stare out the window. Troy Benson stood at her door, the business end of a large handgun aimed at her face.

"Get out," he repeated.

So much for waiting until she heard from Ian.

Jane didn't really mind having to bump up her schedule. The only part that really bothered her was the fact that his gun was seriously larger than hers.

Chapter Four

"Hands up." Troy Benson backed up a step as the driver's side door opened.

The woman slowly raised her hands as she dropped her feet to the ground and pushed out of the vehicle. "I don't know what this is about, mister, but I'm lost. All I need are some directions on how to get to town."

He would just bet she needed directions. "You have some ID?"

She nodded. "In my bag."

He motioned to his right with his weapon. "Step away from the car."

When she'd sidestepped, not taking her eyes off him, to the middle of the road, he reached, equally careful not to take his eyes off her, for the purse sitting on the console inside the vehicle. He closed the door and jerked his head toward the place he called home for now. "This way."

She didn't argue, which surprised him. It shouldn't have. The woman wasn't lost. She had been watching him all afternoon. She'd come into the diner earlier that day.

Leading the way, she walked along the gravel road, then made the left into the dirt driveway leading to the house. Midway down the drive, she hesitated.

"Look." She glanced over her shoulder at him. "I don't want any trouble. I just need to find my aunt's house. She called and I haven't seen her since I was a kid and I don't have a clue where she lives except that it's—"

"Keep moving," he ordered, cutting her off. She could just save all that babble. Whatever she was up to, he would soon know.

As she climbed the rickety steps to his porch, he considered the idea that he should have left already. He had known this was coming. What a damned fool he was. This town didn't mean anything to him. The job damned sure didn't. Still, he hated like hell to pick up and leave. He'd gotten close to a couple of people, as close as he dared anyway.

Stupid. Way stupid.

Anyone close to him was a target. He knew better. But four years had allowed him to lose his edge…to believe it was over.

It would never be over.

The only thing he could do to protect those around him was to get the hell out of here as fast as possible.

At the front door she stopped and faced him defiantly. "Okay, I'm not going in there with you." She stared him straight in the eye. "You'll just have to shoot me here, I guess."

The lady was tall and slim, but not at all helpless or frail looking. In fact, she looked damned determined and fearless for a woman lost on a deserted road.

Troy reached past her and pushed the door open. "I don't know who you are—" he held his aim steady on her chest "—but I do know who you aren't. You aren't lost and you definitely aren't looking for your aunt's house. Now get inside."

A pulse-pounding moment passed with her staring defiantly at him. No way was she some lost stranger. The lady was way too steady, way too in control. Evidently she thought he was as stupid as his recent actions had shown him to be.

"Fine." She executed an about-face and stamped inside. "But I'm warning you, my aunt's expecting me. She'll call the police if I don't show up soon. I left her a message saying I was in the area."

Brave, determined *and smart*. He kicked the door closed behind him. "Sit." He gestured to the sofa.

When she'd taken a seat, he plopped her purse onto the back of the closest chair and dug through it. He tossed the usual female items into the chair's seat. Brush. PDA. Lip balm. He opened her wallet. Jane R. Sutton. Chicago. Twenty-nine. No other forms of ID, no credit cards. One bank check card. A picture of her with an older woman.

"That's my aunt," she piped up. "Like I said, she's expecting me."

He tossed the purse onto the seat with the other stuff, then walked around to sit on the coffee table directly in front of her. That her eyes didn't flare with fear and she didn't draw away with the same confirmed his suspicions.

"Why are you here?"

"I told you—"

"The truth, Ms. Sutton—if that's even your real name," he fired back. "I want the truth now."

She shook her head. Dropped her hands into her lap and shrugged. "You've got problems, mister. Have you seen a shrink about your paranoid delusions?"

He ignored her question. "Who sent you?"

"My mother," she retorted. "She thinks her sister needs help after her surgery. I'm supposed to stay with her a couple of weeks."

She was good. He'd give her that. "Just stop," he warned. "I'm not playing that game with you."

"What game?"

That she could look so innocent only fueled his fury. "I tell you what, Ms. Sutton. I'll tie you up in the basement." He stood. "And when you're ready to tell me the truth, we'll try this again."

There was the widening of eyes he'd anticipated several minutes ago. She did not want to be tied up.

"Wait." She leaned forward a bit. "I'll tell you the truth. Just don't put me in the basement."

He resumed his seat on the coffee table. "Why are you watching me?"

She heaved a big breath. "I'm from the *Trib*. My boss wanted me to get the story on how you rescued Stuart Norcross's wife and son. It's a big story. Maybe you don't realize, but Norcross is—"

"I know who he is." Troy's fury simmered. He should have left the woman and child before the cops arrived. But the woman had been so shaken, her injuries possibly life-threatening, he had been afraid to leave her alone with the child until help arrived.

So much for the good Samaritan bit.

"Then you know that any event, large or small, in his life is big news." She chewed her bottom lip a second. "I need the story. That's all I came for, I swear." She glanced at the gun. "I won't say anything about your lack of social etiquette."

Troy searched Jane Sutton's face, then her eyes,

looking for the lie. It was entirely possible that one of the cops had leaked his description to a reporter friend, especially one as determined and persuasive as this one. She could be telling the truth. But her demeanor, her lack of fear of the weapon in his hand, indicated otherwise. If she was a reporter, she had a background in something else. Yes, Stuart Norcross was a big deal in the social and business pages, but this story wasn't big enough to merit staring down a gun barrel to get.

"If you get your story, you'll leave me alone?" he ventured. "That's all you came here for?"

She nodded. "The readers love hero stories. Especially the ones about ordinary guys who come to the rescue. They'll eat it up."

"And show up at the hero's door wanting autographs and photo ops," he countered.

She shook her head this time. "Oh, I would never leak your location. You have my word on that."

He needed a new strategy. "Where are your press credentials?"

Her right hand moved to the pocket of her slacks.

"Wait. Stand up."

Her brow furrowed with confusion.

"Stand up," he repeated.

Another of those beleaguered sighs accompanied her push up from the sofa.

"Hands back up," he ordered.

She rolled her eyes but obeyed.

He reached into her pocket. She tensed, drew in a sharp breath. Their gazes locked. "Just making sure you don't have any pepper spray tucked in here."

A curt nod had him forcing his fingers deeper into her pocket until he'd found what he was looking for. He pulled out a press badge for the *Chicago Tribune*. After turning the badge over a couple of times, he said, "Looks real enough." He held on to her phone as he resumed his seat.

"So." She sat down on the sofa again. "Do I get the story?"

He thought about the question a moment, settled on his strategy. "Sorry. I don't know what you're talking about." Lowering his weapon, he stood and rounded the coffee table. "You've got the wrong guy."

"Are you kidding me?"

He didn't have to look back to know she was following him to the door. Good, that would make getting her out of his house a little easier.

"Wait." She stalled halfway across the room. "You said you knew what I meant about the story being big."

"I said," he reiterated, "I knew who Norcross was. Anyone who reads the papers would. I know his wife and child were in an accident—that was in the papers, too. But I don't know anything about the guy who rescued them. If you thought that was me, you made a mistake."

Jane Sutton held up both hands stop sign fashion, then waved them back and forth as if to erase his statements. "No way. Mrs. Norcross described you." She glanced at his left arm. "All the way down to the cut on your arm. You got that injury dragging her out of the wrecked car."

He folded his arms over his chest as if that would hide the truth she spoke. "According to the papers, the accident was pretty bad."

"That's right. You should know." She matched his stance. "You were there."

"I would imagine that Mrs. Norcross was panicked and confused. Probably scared to death. Worried about her child. Who knows what the guy who rescued her really looked like? Could've been anyone around here. Folks in this town don't go around bragging about doing the right thing. Or—" he sent her a pointed look "—nosing around for rewards."

Her gaze narrowed. "So if you didn't cut your arm in the rescue, what happened?"

"I'm a short-order cook, lady. I get burned all the time. The diner's equipment is old. Things don't always work right and I have to tear 'em apart to find the problem." He held up his arm. "I cut my arm working on the grill's wiring."

"I don't believe you, Mr. Benson."

"Believe what you like, Ms. Sutton." He opened the door. "Give your aunt my best."

"What about my phone and purse?" Her lips pinched in frustration. "And my press credentials?"

He handed her the phone and press badge, then jerked his head toward the chair. "Take your stuff. And go."

She stalked across the room, shoved her things back into her purse. When she'd slung the strap over her shoulder she glared at him. "For a hero, you're a really rude guy."

"I'm no hero, Ms. Sutton." He studied her profile as she hesitated at the door but refused to look at him. "I'm just a short-order cook trying to get by."

Jane Sutton hesitated one more beat before walking out the open door. She stormed up the drive and to the road. Once she'd made the turn toward where they had left her car he lost sight of her in the dusk.

He hadn't seen the last of the lady.

The other thing he was completely certain of was that he had to get on the road.

What had he been thinking hanging around after that accident?

The paramedics had asked him questions. The two cops had gotten a good look at him before he'd found an opportunity to slip into the woods. Mrs. Norcross had obviously remembered the details far too clearly.

Troy was glad she and her son were okay. No way could he have walked away after witnessing her car going off the road.

If he'd opted to forgo his run that night.

If it hadn't rained so hard so suddenly.

If she hadn't chosen that particular route that particular night.

But she had. And he'd had no choice but to do the right thing.

Now he was left with no choice once more.

If the press, assuming Jane Sutton actually worked for the *Chicago Tribune*, was on to his identity, it wouldn't be long until others learned those details as well.

Troy Benson was finished.

He would have to pick a new name.

A new address.

New job.

But first he had to kill Troy Benson.

That was the hardest part. Finding a way to end

a life without getting caught or leaving too many lingering suspicions.

He could do it.

He'd done it before.

Chapter Five

Jane turned the car around and headed back to the highway.

Troy Benson might have the people in this town believing he was just a short-order cook, but that was so far from the truth she wanted to laugh.

It wasn't so unusual for a guy living out in the country to have a handgun. It wasn't even unusual for him to investigate anyone hanging around his property. But the whole interrogation thing had been totally out of character for the persona he was going for.

The guy had something he seriously wanted to hide.

And it had absolutely nothing to do with avoiding the limelight or a much-earned reward.

Jane got a glimpse of a turnoff she'd noticed earlier and slammed on her brakes. She shoved the gearshift into Reverse and backed up. It looked as if there had once been a driveway here, but it had long ago been overcome by weeds and grass. With a glance in the rearview mirror to ensure that Benson hadn't followed her, she pulled forward a little and backed into the drive. When she'd backed a good enough distance from the road to avoid being spotted, she turned off the headlights and ignition.

Since Mr. Benson was armed, it would be in her best interest to carry her weapon just in case he wasn't so pleasant the next time they met. She reached into the console and retrieved her weapon. After adjusting the interior light so that it didn't come on when she opened the door, she got out and closed her car door as quietly as possible.

Sliding the weapon into her waistband, she listened past the sound of the leaves rustling in the slight breeze. It was getting darker by the minute. Thankfully the moon had appeared and was filtering light through the trees. Another five minutes and she wouldn't need to worry about being spotted when she made her way back to the farmhouse. Since she'd carefully staked out the area earlier today, she knew the most pedestrian-friendly route to stay out of sight and clear of the gravel road.

Keeping a close eye on Benson until she heard back from the print search was imperative. Jane's instincts were shouting at her that the man was planning to disappear. Though she had no evidence to indicate anything in his past would send him running, and certainly nothing about Norcross's interest in him would prompt such a reaction, she could feel Benson's desire to escape. He was not going to hang around long.

His tension had been palpable. He was worried big time about who she was and what her exact intentions might be. Her appearance alone was not nearly enough motivation to prompt him to cut and run. Something else had to be behind the escalating tension.

Headlights turning onto the gravel road had her stepping back into the tree line. The lights going dark while the vehicle still rolled sent her instincts to the next level.

Since it wasn't hunting season and the only inhabited house on this stretch of the road was Benson's, there was every reason to believe this visitor was here for similar reasons as she.

Logic told her this could be an actual reporter attempting to track down the hero who had rescued Norcross's family. But her gut told her differently. So far, no one had the scoop on the anonymous rescuer. At least not that had been reported. Nope, this was no reporter.

This was trouble with a capital *T*.

The sedan stopped short of Benson's drive. The front doors, driver's and passenger's, opened. Despite the dark clothing and the ski masks, the hazy light of the moon allowed her to make out enough about the tall, broad-shouldered frames to recognize that both were male. The driver motioned to the passenger, sending him through the overgrown pasture toward Benson's house.

Damn. Definitely not good.

Jane weaved her way through the dense underbrush, trying to keep noise to a minimum. If she had Benson's number she could warn him.

"Damn it," she muttered under her breath.

If these guys got to his house before she did—

"Don't move."

The barrel pressed to the back of her skull proved far more persuasive than the issued order.

"I...need to borrow a phone," she said, offering the first excuse that came to mind. "My car broke down. I'm totally lost." She could use the aunt story again. The insistent pressure against the back of her head warned that this guy wasn't going to be nearly as amiable as Benson had been.

Using his free hand, he patted her down, took possession of her weapon and phone. "Turn around and start back in the direction of your car."

That he growled the order confirmed her speculation. This guy wasn't going to make this easy.

"Okay, okay." She moved around him and started toward where she'd left her car. "I didn't realize I was trespassing. Chill out. As soon as I can get in touch with AAA I'm out of here."

"Next," he said, giving her a prod with the muzzle of his handgun, "I guess you're going to tell me that you didn't have enough bars on your cell to make the call already."

"How'd you know?" Now she was a comedian. How the hell had she missed this big guy coming up behind her? Her instincts were definitely off tonight. Maybe not off, just too focused on her target.

"Just shut up and keep walking."

Jane kept walking. She still had options. When they reached her car she could make a move. Try and take him down before he could pull off a round.

Risky at best.

Play along and see where it goes from here, particularly if these guys were after Benson for something other than the Norcross rescue as she suspected. They could end up abducted together.

Neither of the two was appealing, but her options were limited.

"I've got her."

The guy with the gun had obviously put in a

call to his cohorts. She considered the fact that she'd only seen two men in the car that had arrived after she pulled off the road. Which likely meant the guy behind her already had Benson under surveillance.

The next logical question was, how had these guys found him?

If Benson had fallen off the radar in a previous life, had these guys been closing in on him already or was finding him somehow related to the Norcross accident? She'd sensed that "being watched" feeling at least once today.

Norcross had come to the Colby Agency, but had he gone to someone else or tried a different avenue first?

There was no reason to suspect Norcross would have an ulterior motive for wanting him found.

As they reached her car, Jane glanced back at the guy behind her. Shorter than his friends. This one, too, had donned a ski mask and dark clothing. Oh yeah. He'd been hanging out in these woods, watching.

He had to have parked on a different road, maybe somewhere on the main road, and walked here. Jane had checked out every possible spot along this gravel road, from one end to the other.

"Facedown on the car," her captor ordered.

She leaned over the truck, facedown as ordered,

arms spread wide. From the edge of her vision she could see him raise the cell phone to his ear.

"What do ya want me to do with her?"

Nice. Nothing like being the excess baggage. Too bad she couldn't hear the guy on the other end of the line.

"Got it."

Jane braced for whatever came next.

Fingers tangled in her hair, jerking her upright. "Come on."

"Ouch! What's the deal, man?" She tried to infuse fear into her voice, but mostly the words came out ticked off.

"The boss has a few questions for you."

At least that meant she wasn't going to eat a bullet just yet. Something to be thankful for.

"What boss?" She stumbled forward as he pushed her toward the road. "I told you I just need to call AAA. Whatever you guys are into is okay with me. I don't want any trouble." She was relatively certain that line wasn't going to work so well this time.

"Tell it to the boss," he growled, keeping her momentum going by thrusting her head forward.

For now it was one against one. When they met up with his pals, she might not get such even odds.

"Wait," she whined. "You're hurting me."

He jerked her head back against his chin. "That's the point," he muttered in her ear.

She rammed her elbow into his ribs. Curled her leg around his and slammed her back into his chest.

He hit the ground with her on top of him. She scrambled away. Grabbed for the gun he'd dropped. His, not hers. Where the hell was hers? There…on the ground not three feet from him.

"Back off," she warned when he made a dive for her. She held the gun with both hands. "Way back."

As he scrambled backward, she snatched up the weapon he'd taken from her. "Give me my cell."

"Get it yourself," he growled.

The phone lay on the ground halfway between them. She wasn't going for it. No way.

"Get up." She pushed to her feet, keeping her aim steady on the bastard. "I said get up," she repeated when he didn't make a move to obey her order.

The smirk on his lips sent the hair on the back of her neck standing on end. She swung around.

Too late.

A hard forearm connected with her temple. She hit the ground.

"Put her in the trunk."

Trying to mentally shake off the stars floating in front of her eyes, she crawled backward to escape the reach of big hands.

A kick to the ribs from the guy she'd taken down sent the burger and fries she'd eaten earlier hurling up her throat.

"Get that bitch in the car now!" the boss shouted.

Fingers tangled in her hair once more, dragged her to her feet. She gagged. Her stomach clenched.

"Move!"

Her head still throbbing and her equilibrium out of reach, she stumbled forward.

She fell to her knees once on the gravel road. The man holding her by the hair dragged her until she was able to scramble back to her feet. Her scalp throbbed.

By the time they got to the sedan, the other thug had opened the trunk.

The jerk hauling her forward shoved her against the back of the car belonging to his buddies. "Get in."

Her arms and legs shaking, she climbed into the trunk. Landed atop a body.

Before the trunk lid closed she got a glimpse of the waitress—Patsy. Eyes and mouth wide open. Definitely dead.

The trunk closed, leaving Jane in darkness.

She fought to control her breathing and the gag reflex. She was pretty sure no ribs were broken, but the pain was damned ugly.

At least now she knew how these guys figured out where Benson lived.

Poor Patsy.

And Jane also now knew that these guys meant business. This was no newspaper or magazine attempting to get the jump on the story.

This was the past, coming back to resolve an old issue.

Think!

First, she needed to determine if this sedan had a trunk lock protection mechanism that prevented accidental lock-ins. Some cars had it, some didn't.

If she was lucky…she felt around, pushed, tugged.

No luck.

"Damn it!"

She tried the backseat. Pushed, kicked. Wouldn't budge.

Jane pushed aside the frantic thoughts that were escalating toward panic.

Think!

Deep breath. Calm your breathing. Focus. Consider your options.

Her attention settled on the dead woman. Most people carried cell phones these days. Would Patsy's still be on her body?

Moving her hands slowly over the woman's torso, she felt in her pockets. Hesitated. Then checked her shirt pocket.

No phone.

"Sorry, Patsy," Jane muttered.

Voices outside drew her attention away from her current situation and the dead woman. She listened hard, tried to make out the conversation.

The men were preparing to move in on Benson. She couldn't determine if their intent was lethal…

She had to get out of this trunk.

As if she'd telegraphed the thought, the trunk lid opened.

"Out!"

"Gladly," she mumbled as she clambered out. Her side hurt like hell. Her head, too.

As soon as her feet hit the ground, the jerk who'd first sneaked up on her grabbed her by the arm. "Unless you want to end up like the smart-mouthed woman in the trunk, you'll do as we say."

Chances were, she'd end up like that anyway. "Just tell me what you want me to do."

One of the other two men grabbed her by the chin and forced her to look at him. "You're going to walk up to Benson's door and tell him about your car trouble. You get him outside and you're done. Free to go."

Yeah, right. "I can do that." She trembled, just to give the impression she was afraid. At their mercy. A quick glance at the automatic weapons the three now sported made the show a hell of a lot easier.

His fingers tightened on her chin. "We will be watching your every move. You won't be able to see us, but we'll be there. Screw this up and we'll shoot you on the spot."

"Got it." Jane swallowed, let go a purposely shaky breath.

He let go of her chin. "Walk her as far as you can. If she makes a run for it, shoot her."

Jerk number one hauled her toward the gravel road. Jane didn't resist. She understood exactly what was going to happen here. For whatever reasons, these guys didn't want to move in on Benson. They wanted him out in the open. An easy target.

Whatever Benson had done in the past, these people wanted him dead. Now. No questions, no special revenge tactics. Just dead.

Just like she would be in about two minutes.

That meant just one thing.

She had to outsmart these jerks.

"Now." The fingers clamped harder on her arm. "You do like he said and you're free to go." The vise on her arm fell away. "Don't make me have to shoot you."

"Whatever you say." Jane turned down the driveway leading to Benson's house.

She smiled even as she imagined the three men fanning out in the tree line, their scopes zeroed in on her back. In four years at Brown University and six years in the military she hadn't once met a man whom she couldn't best.

They had no idea just how much *trouble* she could be.

Chapter Six

Troy was prepared when the knock came at his door.

He couldn't be sure if the woman, Jane Sutton, was working with the others or not, but that didn't really matter at this point.

They had caged him in.

There was nowhere to go without confrontation.

Only one thing to do.

Go down shooting.

He took a breath, leveled the barrel of his weapon. "Come in."

The door opened.

His gaze locked with Jane's.

In that one instant he saw the warning.

She dived for the floor.

Troy pitched right, hit the floor and rolled.

Gunfire erupted.

"There's three of them," Jane said as she scrambled up onto all fours. "You got another weapon?"

Troy cast a you're-kidding look in her direction. As far as he was concerned she was the enemy.

The window above her shattered and she ducked down. "We gotta get outta here."

That much was true.

He rolled to his left and low-crawled into the hall and toward the kitchen.

She crawled after him.

Three feet separated him from the kitchen stairs leading to the second floor. If he was fast enough, with the lights out, he might just make the stairs before whoever was likely out back fired off a round.

He hesitated.

He could leave her.

But if she wasn't with them…they would kill her.

"On my mark," he called back to her, "run."

"Copy."

Had to be ex-military.

"One…" The hail of gunfire escalated. Blowing out the front room lights. "Two…" He braced. "Run!"

He rushed for the stairs.

He'd gotten a mere two steps up and she was on his heels.

Bullets splattered the kitchen cabinets.

By the time he hit the second-floor landing she was questioning his logic.

"I hope this means you have a plan."

"Sort of."

"Perfect."

He wrenched open the door that hid the attic stairs and lunged upward. "Close it behind you."

She did as he said, then double-timed it to catch up to him.

The attic was as dark as pitch. But he knew the way. He reached the window on the west end of the house and climbed out just as the sound of footsteps warned that his enemy had entered the house.

He dropped to the porch roof, a full eight feet, rolled and barely caught himself before going over the edge.

She hit the roof a second later, crashed into him, almost knocking him over that edge.

She looked around, grappling for her bearings.

"Now we jump," he explained before she could ask.

He didn't wait for her response.

He jumped, grunted on impact. Rolled.

She hit the ground next to him. The air whooshed from her lungs. No time for her to catch her breath. He grabbed her by the arm and ran for the woods. The underbrush slowed them down. He pushed harder, kept a desperate grip on her hand. She stumbled once but he didn't let her slow his momentum.

He'd memorized this route, run it most nights.

Half a mile later they broke out of the woods into the old Haines back pasture. Not much cover…had to run faster.

Almost there. He could see the back of the big old barn. Just a little bit farther.

To his surprise, she kept up with him.

Definitely ex-military.

He rounded the barn, let go of her hand and reached for the barn doors. "I have transportation in here."

"I'll get the doors," she said on a gasp for air.

He nodded, rushed between the narrowly open doors.

The old car wasn't much to look at, but it ran like hell. Souped-up V-8 with a four-speed transmission. He'd reworked it himself. He had it gassed up and ready for exactly this moment.

By the time he revved the engine and shifted into Reverse, the doors were open wide. He charged out of the barn, hit the brakes and waited for her to jump in.

He bumped over the rutted road leading from the barn to where the old house used to be. The moonlight spotlighted the relic of a chimney that attested to the fact that a house had once stood in that spot.

"Who the hell were those guys?"

As they entered the main road, a mile beyond his place, she twisted in the seat to stare out the rear window. He didn't answer her question, instead he focused on putting as much distance between them and the shooters as possible. By now the shooters would have realized that he and the woman were no longer on foot. It would take some time for the men to reach their car and give chase, but give chase they would.

"Friends of yours?" she commented as she turned around and reached for the seat belt. She stared at the lap belt. No shoulder harness.

"I could ask you the same thing." He kept his attention on the road. "They showed up about the same time you did."

"Do you have a cell phone?"

She planned to ignore his roundabout question, did she?

"Yes, I have a cell phone."

"I need to call in."

"You mean *call your aunt?*"

She heaved a disgusted breath. "I just need to use your phone, okay?"

He shot her a look then. "Lady, I don't know who you are, but I do know that I'm not that crazy."

"I'm not with those guys, Benson." She peered at the upcoming road sign. "Where are we headed?"

"We," he said pointedly, "aren't headed any-where. I'm dropping you off in town. There's a pay phone at the convenience store down the block from the diner. You can *call in* from there."

That she sat in silence after his announcement was not a good sign. He'd only just met this lady, but he didn't take her for the type to give up so easily.

What was her game?

Not his problem. He didn't have time to wonder or to worry. Worrying about others always got him into trouble.

Losing the shooters back at his house was his problem.

That meant starting over.

Four years lost.

"Look, Mr. Benson, I'm not with those guys back there," she said again. "I don't know why they showed up guns blazing, but I was just as surprised as you were."

Arguing with her was a waste of energy. Since he would need to drive all night he didn't have any energy to waste. They were almost to town. He was dropping her off, end of story. No way was she making any calls while she was still with him.

He slowed for the turn onto South Street. A few more blocks and he was out of here.

The Sack-N-Go was still open. Good. She could make her call and wait inside. Those guys weren't going to risk causing trouble where the police might be called in. His place was one thing, in the middle of nowhere with no close neighbors. The middle of town—even one as small as Plano—would present far too much potential for trouble.

In his experience with these types, they didn't want to draw attention.

She would be safe here.

He pulled into the parking lot and braked to a stop by the pay phone.

He turned to his passenger. "This is your stop."

She stared directly at him. The neon sign provided ample light to see the questions in her eyes. "Why are those men after you?"

"It's a long story, Ms. Sutton. I think you'll understand when I say I don't really have time to go into it right now."

Another of those prolonged moments of silence.

He had to get moving. But she just kept looking at him with those brown eyes filled with worry.

Why the hell would she be worried about him?

"I can help you."

Was she for real?

"The way you can help me at the moment is to get out of the car and go inside until the dust settles." He kept one eye on the rearview mirror. If they suspected he'd headed this way…

"I work for the Colby Agency. Trust me, we can help you."

He hated to do it this way. Reaching for his weapon, he gave her one more chance. "Get out of the car."

She glanced at the gun. "Suit yourself. It's your life."

Actually, no…it wasn't.

His life had ended four years ago.

Jane Sutton got out of his car and stalked to the pay phone.

Maybe in the last four years he'd grown stupid. But for some ridiculous reason he suddenly felt as if he'd let his one chance walk away.

"Right."

He'd definitely gone stupid.

Shoving the stick into Reverse, he eased off the clutch and rolled backward.

Headlights appeared at the end of the block.

Troy held his breath.

Could be a local.

Could be someone passing through.

The sedan took a sudden left, roaring into the Sack-N-Go parking lot.

Troy shifted into First.

The passenger side door opened.

"Go!" she shouted as she dived into the seat.

There was no time to argue.

He blasted out of the parking lot.

The sedan squealed out behind him.

He had a plan.

A route for this very scenario.

He roared through the gears, propelling the car forward and leaving his tail behind.

A left. Then a right. Another right.

Around behind the high school.

One rapid turn after the other.

Until he reached Route 34.

Once on the highway, he focused on gaining speed and eating up the asphalt.

Five minutes, then ten passed with no sign of headlights in the rearview mirror.

Troy relaxed.

He would lie low for the night and figure out his next move in the morning.

This exit strategy had been planned for four years, but as time had passed he'd begun to believe he wouldn't need it.

Complacency was the true enemy. He knew this all too well. Still he'd let it happen.

Nothing he could do about it now.

Except move on. Do what he had to do.

"Why are those men after you?"

She just wasn't going to stop asking that same question. He mentally altered his longtime getaway plan.

Step one, get rid of his company.

He sent a look her way. "Who sent you to find me?" he asked instead of answering her question.

"Stuart Norcross. He wanted to show his gratitude for what you did for his wife and son."

Troy shook his head. He couldn't regret what he'd done or even call it a mistake. But that one act had sure as hell wrecked his existence.

The real question was, since his name hadn't appeared in any of the reports related to the Norcross rescue, what or who had tipped off his pursuers?

"What methods did you use for finding me?" He checked the rearview mirror once more despite being fairly certain he was in the clear.

"Mrs. Norcross's description. I asked around town."

That wouldn't have alerted the sleeping dragon.

"That's it?" He sent her a skeptical look.

"That's it."

Didn't make sense.

The fact was it didn't make any difference in the end.

He made a right and drove the final few miles to the place he'd hoped never to have to use.

The house was deserted. Condemned actually.

He parked the car behind the run-down house.

Maybe he was getting older. Maybe he was just tired. Troy closed his eyes. He did not want to do this again.

"They're not going to give up. Running will just delay the inevitable."

He opened his eyes. She shouldn't be here. Damn, but he'd screwed up.

"The Colby Agency can help you."

She'd said that before. But she had no idea. No idea at all what she was getting into.

He opened the door and got out. Drew in a deep breath of night air. As much as he hated to admit it, he was going to miss this place. A world away from the past.

The car door closing dragged his attention to the woman. He still had to get rid of her. But not tonight. Tonight he had to lie low. Make a plan.

"I'm not a big fan of one-sided conversations," she noted aloud.

He walked around the car to the trunk. Shoved the keys in the lock and opened it.

There was only one sleeping bag. A flashlight, a couple of bottles of water and some granola bars.

He hadn't expected company.

With a firm thud he closed the trunk and headed to the back door of the rickety old house. He rifled through the keys on the ring until he found the right one. When he had the door open, he switched on the flashlight. No electricity. No running water. No bathroom. Not much of anything. Just a roof, such as it was, and a floor for the night.

One stop in the morning and he was out of here.

He turned back to Sutton, stepped inside and held the door for her.

Maybe she would come in handy after all.

He couldn't afford to show his face around town.

But she could pull it off without a hitch.

He'd never been one to believe that anything happened for a reason. A man made his way in life, the good and the bad.

But maybe he'd been wrong.

Maybe Jane Sutton had shown up for a reason.

Chapter Seven

The telephone rang.

Victoria froze.

What if Jim and Tasha had run into trouble? They could have been detained. Injured.

Or worse.

Fear slithered up her spine.

"Victoria."

She turned to Merri Walters, the agency investigator assigned to Victoria and Jamie's interior security. Deep breath. *Don't let the worry turn to paranoia.* "Yes, Merri."

"Slade just informed me that a sedan headed for this address has passed through the property gate."

Slade Conroy was another new member of the Colby Agency staff. How many new recruits had

Ian and Simon hired the beginning of the year, five? No, six. "Thank you, Merri." Victoria hesitated a moment before moving toward the phone. "Have you been able to reach Jane yet?"

"No, ma'am. Riley Porter is on his way to Plano to see if he can locate her."

This was troubling. Losing touch with an investigator was never indicative of anything good. But Jane Sutton, former army intelligence officer, was as highly trained as anyone.

The phone rang for the fifth time.

"Would you like me to get that?"

Victoria shook her head. This was her home. She had to pull herself together. "Please get the door when Slade clears our visitor."

"Yes, ma'am."

Merri moved to the foyer as Victoria crossed the room and picked up the phone. "Hello." Her voice sounded strained.

"Victoria."

Lucas. Thank God. "I was hoping to hear from you tonight." She cradled the receiver as if she could touch the voice of her husband coming across the line.

"I'm sorry it took me so long to get to you."

Victoria's brow lined with confusion. She looked at the phone. It sounded as if…he were right here in the room with her.

She turned around. Lucas stood in the doorway, Merri right behind him. He closed his cell phone and opened his arms.

Victoria dropped the phone and ran into her husband's arms.

"I'll check on Jamie," Merri said as she backed out of the room after picking up the phone Victoria had dropped.

Everything would be fine now. Victoria needn't worry anymore.

Lucas was home.

Her husband drew back and smiled at her. "How's our girl?"

The relief was so enormous that Victoria found drawing in her next breath difficult. "She's sleeping. This is all a big game to her. Jamie thinks Merri is her new best friend."

Lucas smiled. Those gray eyes shimmered with the love that took Victoria's breath all over again. How she had missed this man.

"I'm so glad you're home." She pulled him close again, held on tightly. "I've been so afraid." Lucas was the one person to whom she could admit her deepest fears.

Lucas cupped her face, kissed her lips. "Come," he murmured. "Let's have a glass of wine and sit before the fire."

She laughed as he took her hand in his. "But it's July."

Lucas winked. "I don't think we'll notice."

Victoria watched as her husband meticulously selected a bottle of wine. She gathered two stemmed glasses and the corkscrew, then followed him to the den.

As he closed the double doors, she arranged their glasses on the table before the sofa. He strolled toward her, his trademark limp only making him look stronger, sexier. Leaning down, he picked up the remote on the table next to the sofa and set the flames of the gas logs to low, just enough of a dancing flicker to lend the desired ambiance.

Then he removed his jacket. She folded it neatly, held it close and breathed deeply of his scent before placing it on the arm of the sofa. She loved the way he smelled, the subtle, earthy essence of his cologne. When he'd loosened his tie, he skillfully opened the bottle of wine. Victoria picked up one glass for him to fill, then the other. He set the bottle aside and accepted one of the glasses.

"To us." He touched his glass to hers. "No one is going to harm us or those we love."

Victoria sipped her wine, fought back the uncertainty. Lucas had never, ever let her down. She had never before allowed herself to feel so…afraid.

She'd always been strong, stood tall…refused to be intimidated.

Perhaps age was to blame.

"I can read your mind, Victoria."

Those gray eyes searched hers. "Can you, Lucas? I knew your skills were vast and noteworthy, but mind reading? I believe you'll need to convince me of that one."

He smiled, and the sheer charisma of it prompted her heart into a faster rhythm.

"You're doubting yourself." He leaned down, placed his glass next to the wine bottle on the coffee table. "You've worked so hard for so very long to protect everyone around you that you're feeling weary…uncertain if you can protect those who need you most at this juncture."

Her lips slid into a smile. "I see. You do, indeed, read minds."

He took her glass and placed it next to his. Then he cradled her face in both hands. "Not really. I just know my wife."

"This has been difficult," she confessed. "I keep remembering those final days before Jim was taken. Jamie's almost the same age he was. I keep analyzing my every step then and now. Wondering if I could have done anything differently then. If I'll make the same mistakes this time."

Saying the words aloud was like lifting a boulder from her chest.

"You—" he peered into her eyes, his urging her to trust his words "—did nothing wrong, Victoria. The past is over. Don't keep revisiting that horror. Focus on the present. On the future. We will protect Jamie and we'll get this son of a bitch, no matter what it takes."

She nodded. "You're right. I just hope Jim and Tasha don't take too many risks trying to get home."

The pad of his thumb stroked her cheek. "I sent two of my specialists in to help with their exodus. I received word just before I arrived that contact has been made. Jim and Tasha should be on a plane headed home in a few hours."

"Thank you, Lucas." Relief made her weak. Lucas was right, with the specialists involved, she had no reason to worry. The specialists were an elite team, operated under the CIA's shadow unit, Mission Recovery. They could get in and out of anywhere with little or no incident.

"Jamie is safely tucked in her bed under the watchful eye of Merri," Lucas went on. "And you and I have this exquisite bottle of wine and that lovely fire all to ourselves."

Lucas pulled her down to the sofa, handed her the glass of wine, then retrieved his own. They drank it slowly, stealing kisses between each sweet sip. She felt safe...whole with Lucas home. With each touch of his lips she felt her strength and courage fortifying.

Soon they set the glasses aside. Lucas locked the door, took his time crossing back to her. She watched as he unbuttoned his shirt. Desire sang through her veins. Too many days had passed since she'd been in this man's arms...her body pressed against his.

She needed him.

Together they would get through this.

Chapter Eight

Outside Plano, Illinois, 10:15 p.m.

Benson stepped back and surveyed his work with the flashlight. He'd spread the sleeping bag in the middle of the floor. "You can have the sleeping bag."

"Where will you sleep?" It wasn't cold by any means, but sleeping on the bare floor at this place wouldn't be an option. Not only was the house falling in, but years of dust, dirt and decay layered every square inch.

"I'll sleep in the car."

Jane knew how that would go. She would wake up and he'd be gone. "I'll take the backseat." No way was she letting him out of her sight.

He turned the flashlight's beam on her face. She blinked at the brightness.

"It's too dangerous," he argued. "They could track us to this place. If they find me out there, they won't bother looking for you in here. It's me they want."

She set her hands on her hips. "Who is *they*, Benson? Considering we're sort of in this together, I think I have a right to know what's going on."

Fury tightened his features. Though the light's beam was focused on her, his face was lit plenty well enough for her to see that her lack of cooperation wasn't making him happy in the least.

"The less you know the better off you'll be."

Now, there was an original line. "They know who I am, Benson. If they don't catch up with you, they're going to hunt me down and demand to know what I know. I don't think it'll be pretty."

He turned his back on her then.

"And even if they have their way with you, I'm a witness. A loose end. Getting rid of me would be in their best interest." She walked up behind him. "The Colby Agency can help you. All you have to do is let us in. What's your story?"

He faced her once more, this time the flashlight directed at the floor, leaving them in a spotlight of sorts. "If I tell you who I am and the Colby Agency starts digging around in my past, the situation will only escalate. This isn't as simple as the good guys versus the bad guys. As a matter of fact, I'm pretty sure, in this instance, there are no good guys."

"There're always good guys, Benson. All you have to do is determine who they are. Lucky for you—" she folded her arms over her chest "—you're looking at one."

He stared at her for a long moment without responding. "I'll sleep on it."

Jane threw her hands up. "Do you have that luxury?" She really, really needed to check in with the agency to see if anything had come back on the print check. Victoria and the others would be worried that she hadn't called in, and if they'd been trying to reach her, as she suspected they had, the worry would increase with each passing hour she was out of touch. "I would think time would be your enemy under the circumstances."

The stare-off continued. "Time, Ms. Sutton, is all I have, and all I ever have is the moment."

The regret or maybe the sadness that etched across his face with that statement tugged at her. *Living for the moment* was a great line when selling vacations and leisure items such as boats and beer, but it was no way to live on a daily basis.

"If nothing else," she prodded, "talk to me. Tell *me* about yourself. Your real name, where you came from. We're in this together, Benson," she added quickly when he literally took a step back. "Neither of us may have the luxury of tomorrow. Talk to *me*."

There was a long, long pause. Jane had just about given up on an answer when he finally spoke.

"You tell me about you and I'll tell you as much as I can about me."

Fair enough. "I can do that." The weariness hit her all at once. As if the kick to her ribs and the whop to the side of her head, along with the run-for-your-life sprint, had waited until now to take their toll. She took a seat on the sleeping bag. "I was born in a suburb of Chicago. Went off to Brown University to pursue my parents' hope that I would become the greatest lawyer Chicago has ever seen."

She tamped down the emotion that even seven years later still formed a lump in her throat when she dwelled on the subject of her father. "After a long battle with cancer, my father died in my senior year. It took every penny of the life insurance he had to settle his medical expenses and pay the mortgage on the family home. My mother had always been a stay-at-home mom and suddenly at fifty she had no way to support herself and no marketable skills. So I went from Brown to the good old U.S. Army and I've been taking care of my mother since."

He took a cautious step in her direction. "That was your mom in the photo with you?"

She nodded.

"Your mom's a lucky lady to have a daughter like you."

Jane shrugged. "I'm the lucky one. My mom's the best." She looked him directly in the eye. "What about your family?"

He moved the flashlight to a position that worked more like a lamp, providing some light in the room but not nearly enough to read those blue eyes. Then he sat down on the other end of the sleeping bag.

"My parents were killed in a boating accident when I was a kid. But the few memories I have of them are good ones."

"Who took care of you after your folks died?" She had a soft spot for abandoned kids. Had to be horrifying to be left totally alone and helpless.

"My uncle."

The change in his tone told her instantly that there was no love lost between him and his uncle. "No brothers and sisters?"

He shook his head.

Jane was an only child, too. It made for bouts of loneliness now and then. But she and her mom had always been close and she'd had plenty of good friends.

"Any cousins?" Surely his uncle had kids.

"Oh yeah." He looked away. "But none I want to talk about."

Ah. So the trouble was with the uncle and the cousins. "Where'd you grow up?"

His gaze collided with hers. "There are some things I can't tell you."

She nodded. "I understand. Is where you grew up one of them?"

"I suppose not. Silver Springs, Maryland."

They were moving in the right direction. "College?"

He laughed, but the sound was dry. "Ten years to be exact. Yale."

She couldn't help herself, the laugh burst from her chest. "Are you serious?"

He didn't have to answer and she didn't have to see the full depth of the tension in his eyes. She could feel it radiating off him.

"So, you're what, a doctor?"

"Research scientist."

"What kind of research?"

"Off-limits."

"Okay, okay." College for ten years, he had to have worked for a few years. What did that make him? Thirty-something? "Ever been married?"

"Off-limits."

That was a yes. "Kids?"

"No."

She started to ask her next question when he asked, "Why did you leave the military? Obviously you didn't have a problem with the physical challenges."

Definitely not. "My mother's health deteriorated and I was all she had. So I took a hardship discharge and moved back home."

"Not married?"

That one drew a burst of laughter that, like his, held no humor. "Afraid not. I guess I'm just not the type men see as a wife."

Troy recognized that he'd hit upon a sensitive spot. Though he didn't see why. "What does that mean? You're smart, cute."

"Cute?" She shook her head. "Get real, Benson. I'm not cute."

So maybe cute was the wrong thing to say. "I mean, you're attractive. Maybe you're too liberated to become some guy's ball and chain."

"Boy, you know how to sweet-talk a gal, Benson."

Damn. Had it really been so long since he'd carried on a normal conversation that he no longer knew how? "You seem quite…willful."

Another of those laughs burst from her lips. He liked the way she laughed. It sounded womanly and honest.

"I am quite willful. Determined. Intelligent.

Good at my job." She shrugged. "And all those other things guys don't typically like. Despite your very kind compliment, I'm also just plain Jane. No frills. No glam whatsoever."

He'd noticed she didn't wear makeup. Now that he considered her manner of dress, she was right. No frills. Just practical. "What's wrong with being good at what you do and all those other things?" As a *guy*, he didn't have a problem with that.

"Absolutely nothing." She pulled her knee to her chest and propped her elbow there. "It's the guys who have a problem, not me."

"The Colby Agency is a private investigations firm?" He resisted the hope that attempted to swell. The best attorney in the D.C. area hadn't been able to help him. The police hadn't been able to help him. There was no way in hell some PI agency from Chicago was going to have a shot at clearing up his past.

The past wouldn't go away until he was dead…again.

"The best in the business," Jane assured him. "Clients come from all over the country. Victoria Colby-Camp never lets a client down. Whatever their trouble, she finds the resolution."

Anything that sounded too good to be true generally was. "I think it's way too late for me." He pushed up. Didn't want to talk anymore. Everything he learned about her past just showed him how glaringly screwed up his was. Listening to the hope in her voice when she spoke of the Colby Agency only made him wish for things he couldn't have. Bad business all the way around. What was, was. He'd gotten used to that…

Until she showed up.

She moved up behind him. "It's never too late as long as you're breathing."

He turned to her, wanted to tell her she didn't know what the hell she was talking about, but he knew a brick wall when he hit one. "Bottom line, Ms. Sutton, trouble showed back up in my life right after you did. I'm not one to believe in coincidences. Maybe your agency is not as good as you believe it is."

Her head moved side to side with certainty. "No way. The Colby Agency would never put anyone's life at risk, not even if the person was presumed to be a bad guy. That's not the way we do business."

Someone sure as hell had outed him. If his name and photo hadn't been in the papers, and to his knowledge it had not, then his uncle's men showing up was related to one thing—Jane Sutton.

And the Colby Agency.

Chapter Nine

4:00 a.m.

The cell phone vibrated against his chest.

Troy roused…felt for the phone.

He answered without thinking. "Hello."

"Troy! What's going on?"

He blinked, scrubbed a hand over his face. That was when he realized where he was.

And what had happened.

He turned to the woman lying next to him. Jane Sutton still slept soundly.

The shooters.

He couldn't go home, couldn't go back to the diner.

"Ellen?" He sat up, pushed to his feet. "What's wrong?" Though he'd been half asleep when he answered, the tone of her voice had been several octaves higher than usual. She was upset. "What time is it?"

"Troy, Patsy's dead." She made a sobbing sound.

"What?" He rammed his fingers through his hair. The answer exploded in his chest before his coworker could answer. They'd gotten to Patsy. A sweet, free spirit of a woman who never hurt anyone.

"They found her at your house. The place was all shot up and ransacked. What the hell happened? Where are you? Everyone's worried. You didn't come to work. The sheriff came here looking for you and told us about your house…and Patsy."

A new kind of terror lit in his veins. They could be forcing Ellen to make this call.

"Ellen, are you all right? Is anyone there…who might hurt you?"

"What? No. I'm at the diner. Everyone's worried sick. Most of us have been squalling our eyes out over Patsy. What happened, Troy? I know you couldn't have hurt her. But the sheriff says you're a suspect."

Resignation settled on Troy's shoulders. "Ellen, listen to me. There are people after me who will hurt you if they think you know anything about me. They're the ones who hurt Patsy. Don't tell anyone you've spoken to me. Stay away from my house and watch your back."

She wanted to know what he was going to do and if he was coming back to work. He couldn't answer any of those questions. He ended the call. Closed his phone and shoved it into his pocket.

Dear God. Someone else had died because of him.

"What's going on?"

He turned. Jane Sutton stood near the sleeping bag, her eyes searching his face, looking for clues to what the call had been about.

Could he trust her? Would involving anyone else in this situation help or just create another target?

"That was one of the waitresses from the diner. Those men killed one of my coworkers."

"Patsy."

The name was scarcely a whisper.

"You knew?" Why the hell hadn't she told him?

"When they shoved me in the trunk—" Jane moistened her lips "—she was in there…dead. I should have told you." She closed her eyes and shook her head. "But so much happened I…" When her eyes opened once more, her gaze locked with his. "I guess the truth is I knew you'd be upset and you looked like you had enough to deal with last night."

He stalked over to her. "You didn't think I needed to know something like that?"

"What could you have done about it?"

He didn't want to hear that excuse. She should have told him.

"She was dead, Benson. They probably forced her to lead them to your house and then killed her. There wasn't anything you could have done."

"Except give them what they wanted."

"What is it they want?"

His gaze swung back to hers. "Me."

Jane ran both hands through her sleep-mussed hair, glanced around the dilapidated room. "It's time, Benson." She looked directly at him then. "To tell me the rest of the story so I can help you."

"It's time for me to get on the road. The sheriff thinks I had something to do with Patsy's murder." He planted his hands on his hips. "I can't be taken into custody. They'll have me extradited back to D.C. and then it's over. They win."

"Then I'm going with you." She crouched down to roll up the sleeping bag. "You can't do this alone."

He started to argue, but for the first time in four years he realized one undeniable truth: he needed help. Maybe he should have trusted someone a long time ago. Maybe things wouldn't have come to this…an innocent woman was dead.

Four years ago he had picked Plano, Illinois, a nice quiet town where nothing ever happened, to resurrect his existence. His selfish desire to live had cost Patsy the rest of her life.

He wasn't worth the price she had paid.

While Jane packed up, Troy checked the backyard, then the front. The road was deserted like always. Most of the land belonged to a farmer whose house was on another road that ran parallel to this one. What Troy needed was a different vehicle. They would be looking for his souped-up old junker.

If they could get close enough to Grissom Spring Road, maybe Jane's car would still be there. Unless the cops had towed it. Or the shooters had vandalized it somehow.

It was worth a shot.

In the house Jane grabbed the flashlight and bedroll. She jogged out to the car and tossed both into the backseat. She closed the door and had started to head off in search of Benson when she spotted his cell phone on the front seat charging.

She really, really needed to call in. She also needed to check on her mom.

Jane glanced at first one corner of the house and then the other. No sign of Benson.

She slid into the passenger seat and grabbed the phone. As much as her daughterly instincts urged her to call her mom, if she only got the opportunity to make one call it had to be to the agency. Someone would contact her mother if necessary.

The first ring echoed in Jane's ear. She scanned the yard, hoping to see Benson first in the gloom of dawn. Having him see her first would put a serious damper on the trust she was attempting to build.

"Michaels."

"Ian, it's Jane." She surveyed the yard once more. "Any word back on the prints?"

"Yes, but first, are you safe?"

"For now."

"We heard about the shoot-out at Benson's home. What do you know about the one casualty?"

"The shooters must have used her to find Benson."

"We had surmised as much. Are you still armed?"

Jane hated the answer she had no choice but to give. "No, but Benson is."

"Be very careful with Benson until we have the whole story. He may be dangerous. At this point all we know for sure—"

The driver's-side door opened. Strong fingers manacled around her hand and snatched the phone away. Her gaze locked with Benson's. Even in the twilight there was no missing the fury blazing there.

"Get out of the car," he ordered.

Jane had taken the risk. Now she had to face the consequences. She got out. "I know how this looks," she began.

"Who did you call?" The way he was looking around signaled that he expected the worst.

"My agency. But I—"

"Did you give them our location?" he snarled across the top of the car.

"No." Damn. Three or four giant steps back. "I didn't tell them anything other than the fact that I was with you."

"Anything else?" His broad shoulders shook with outrage.

She shook her head. "Nothing. Ian Michaels, my boss, wanted to know who killed Patsy. I told him it was the shooters who came after you. That's all we had time to discuss." She glared at Benson.

He may be dangerous.

Ian had issued that warning for a reason. He wasn't the kind of man to overreact. Whatever they had learned, it was volatile and grounded in fact.

"Can they use my number to track our location?"

She'd hoped he wouldn't think of that. "There's no reason for them to. I never indicated that—"

"Answer the question," he demanded.

"It's possible." That could seal her fate. "If they

chose to, there are variables, as I'm sure you know, that may or may not be successful."

"What can I do about that?" The fury now throbbed in his jaw.

He didn't have to say *besides shake the hell out of you.* She understood he was furious with her.

"Turn off your phone. Take the battery out." She had to tell him the truth. No matter that the answer put her at greater risk. If there was any chance he suspected there were ways to sever the connection the call had initiated…she had to win back some of the ground she'd lost.

He shut the phone down. Took the battery out and shoved each into a separate pocket. His attention settled on her. "Get in the car."

At least she wasn't out completely.

As they set out on the road, Jane tried again to reassure him. "I swear, I didn't say anything. I just let them know that we were okay. I should have asked first. I was wrong not to. But I have an obligation to my employer."

He just drove for a while. Didn't respond. The way his fingers clutched the steering wheel, it was clear he was still angry.

She'd just about given up on him speaking to her again any time soon when he said, "No matter what you say, Ms. Sutton…"

They were back to the Ms. Sutton thing again.

"They didn't just suddenly find me. They followed you here."

He'd likely spent the entire night dissecting the events of yesterday. He'd come to the only logical conclusion. And maybe he was right. She couldn't prove he was wrong. She had only one defense.

"I can guarantee you that no one in the Colby Agency leaked where I was coming or who I was looking for."

"There's no other way."

A few more miles of asphalt disappeared behind them before he brought up the subject once more. She damned sure wasn't about to broach it again until she thought of something equally logical to his conclusion.

"Four years," he said softly, "I was here four years and they didn't find me. If your agency or Mr. Norcross weren't responsible, then how?"

Right there was the answer. "First off, Mr. Norcross didn't have any idea who you were. Not your name, address, only your description. The Colby Agency reacted to his request. We had no information other than what he gave us. I approached my investigation quite logically. I laid out a search grid based on reasoning that since you were on foot that night you likely lived within a certain radius.

Then I asked around. Locals. The guy in the grocery store. The pharmacist. People like that. That's how I found you."

He made an abrupt turn at the next intersecting county road. "You didn't pass around one of those sketches or anything like that?"

"No. In a rural area like this I didn't think it was necessary."

He made another of those turns without giving a signal.

"What you're saying doesn't add up. They got the word I was here."

"I agree, but it didn't come from the Colby Agency or Norcross. Stuart Norcross had no clue who you were. There's nothing in the system on a Troy Benson."

He may be dangerous.

Then she knew. Merri had left Plano with the bowl at approximately five-thirty. An hour or so to Chicago. If Ian's friend had entered the prints into the system by sevenish…that would mean Benson's fingerprints were flagged and someone had moved damned fast to get men here within the hour.

That was way too iffy. Not enough time. Benson had said he was from the D.C. area. His enemy, assuming that enemy was in D.C., couldn't possibly have gotten his henchmen here that quickly.

Unless he'd used hired guns already in the Chicago area.

Maybe this was her fault. The agency's fault.

She needed more information. She needed to know exactly what he was running from.

Wait.

If Benson's fingerprints were flagged, and the shooters came after him based on that information, they would have known the alias he was using. Finding his home address would have been simple. Killing someone wouldn't have been necessary.

She turned to Benson. "It had to be Patsy."

He sent her a glare. "What're you talking about?"

"Why would they have killed Patsy otherwise?" Made perfect sense. "If they followed me to you, why abduct and murder Patsy?"

The silence that followed told her he was weighing her deduction.

"Did she know that you'd rescued a woman and child from an accident?" Jane turned in her seat to watch his profile. The sun was up now, she could see every angle and valley. Nice face. Even when he was angry.

"She stitched up my arm." He blew out a breath.

"She used to be a nurse's aid or something. I tried to do it myself but I was making a hell of a mess. She came over to my house that night. I told her there was an accident and I got hurt helping the victims. That's all."

He'd just told Jane a lot more than he realized. "Were you and Patsy involved…?" She didn't have to say the rest. He knew what she meant.

"No." Another of those weary sighs. "She wanted to date but I couldn't get involved. I couldn't take the risk."

"I need your phone."

He looked at her as if she'd lost her mind.

"It's the only way to know for sure."

"You're not calling your agency."

"It'll take one minute, I swear. Then I'll hang up again."

He surrendered the phone. "Put it on speaker."

Well, there went her chance of learning what Ian had discovered with the prints. "Okay." She put through the call.

"Michaels."

"Ian, this is Jane. I have you on speaker. Benson and I have a question for you."

Ian's hesitation warned that he was assessing the next step. "Go ahead."

"Can you have research run a check on the

papers in the surrounding area to see if anything else has been run on the Norcross accident?"

"Research has been keeping tabs. I wanted to pass along this new data earlier, but our call was cut short."

Jane glanced at Benson, who didn't look the slightest bit repentant that he'd snatched the phone from her.

"There was an article in one of the online news outlets yesterday. The article showed a picture of the good Samaritan and mentioned Plano. Simon questioned the journalist but he refused to name his source. Not an hour after Simon's visit the journalist made a call to Patsy Wagner to ask why a private investigations firm would be following up on the article she'd sourced for him."

"Thanks, Ian." Jane was glad to have that cleared up.

"Mr. Benson."

The driver's posture stiffened when Ian addressed him directly. Jane resisted the urge to hit the end-call button. Ian had no way of knowing where she was with gaining his trust. Her boss's main concern for now would be her safety.

"I'm certain Ms. Sutton has told you that the Colby Agency can help. You have my word, this agency's word, that we can fulfill any offer or guarantee she makes."

"I'll keep that in mind," Benson said before taking the phone from her hand and ending the call.

"Just so you know," Jane offered, "Ian Michaels is a former U.S. Marshal and Simon Ruhl is former FBI. I don't know what kind of trouble you faced four years ago, but they have extensive connections."

"If you're trying to make your case," Benson turned to her, "you're losing ground. The bureau or anyone associated with the bureau is the last place I would go for help."

Chapter Ten

"Where are we?" Jane scanned the wooded area, which looked exactly like most of the others they'd passed on the back roads Benson had taken.

"We're going to get your car."

"Is that wise?" Since he was already getting out of the car, the question was pretty much irrelevant.

"About as wise," he said as she rounded the car and met him near the trunk, "as continuing to drive around in this old clunker."

He had a point. The old clunker, as he called it, stood out, that was for sure. Her rented sedan was more than a little generic in make and color. But getting to it could be tricky. Especially if any of the reunion party from yesterday was still hanging around. And that was a logical conjecture.

"Straight through there." He pointed east. "You

left your car at the old burned-out house. If the cops didn't spot it, it should still be there."

She'd left the keys in the ignition; the rental could be anywhere by now.

As if he'd read her mind, he asked, "Keys in the car?"

"Yeah." She hadn't expected to be leaving it overnight. Actually, she hadn't expected to be leaving it at all.

"If it's still there, I'll circle back around and pick you up."

Like she was going to trust him to do that. "It's my car," she offered, "I'll go after it. Considering the police are after you, I'll be less of a target than you." Chances were, he intended to be rid of her as soon as possible. Like now.

"I think your logic's a little flawed." He opened the trunk of the old car. "Besides, this is my mess, not yours."

He pulled a second handgun from the trunk and passed it to her. "Keep your eyes open."

To say she was surprised that he gave her a weapon would be a colossal understatement. "You sure you trust me with this?" She checked the clip; full.

"Just stay put," he ordered. "If you hear gunfire, drive back to Plano and go to the police."

"There's this technique," she countered, "maybe

you've heard of it. It's called backup. Ironically, it works most of the time."

His glare was lethal. "I said stay put. I'll bring your car here. You have *my* word."

So he expected her to trust him. Another irony. "I'm a pretty fast runner, as you learned last night." She jerked her head toward the woods. "If we run into trouble that we can't handle, I'll come back here and go for the police."

Frustration scrunched across his forehead. "Are you always this argumentative?"

"Only when confronted with irrational stubbornness."

"Stay behind me."

There was nothing like winning. "Whatever you say."

He shot her another of those looks. Damn, the guy was seriously good looking. Even after sleeping on a filthy floor and going without a shower.

Maybe it was getting that bump on the head that had her obsessing on his good looks. Or the kick in the ribs that was as sore as hell this morning.

The underbrush was thick here. She stayed close on his heels. He knew the way, she didn't. The sun trickled through the leaves, showering interesting shapes of light on the tree trunks and foliage.

When they were on the road again, she hoped to

get him talking. Since Ian hadn't been able to fill her in, she needed everything she could get from Benson. Running wasn't the answer to his problems. Maybe he'd buy himself some more time by disappearing again. But for long-term quality of life, the truth had to come out—the past faced and conquered.

She'd gained enough of his trust for him to arm her, but would it be enough to get him talking?

He held up a hand. She stopped. She couldn't see beyond his broad shoulders, but nothing around her looked familiar. But then, it had been dark last night when she'd parked. And trees, well, they were trees. These looked just like the others they'd passed on the road and had run through last night.

Lowering to a crouch, he waited for her to do the same. Once she hovered next to him, he gestured to his right. "I'm going around and up, closer to the road to move toward your car. You stay here, behind cover. Once I'm in the car and moving, head back. You're close enough to hear the engine start."

"The police could be nearby," she reminded him. "They're looking for you. I can verify that you didn't kill Patsy. Are you certain—" she searched his eyes "—that you don't want to go that route? Whatever happened in the past, if you're innocent, the police will have to be involved at some point."

"Once you hear the engine start, move fast," he

said, totally ignoring her warning. "It won't take me long to get back to where we left the clunker."

She watched him go. Damn, she needed her phone. It would be enormously helpful if she had the information Ian had learned. She had no bargaining chips with this guy. No leverage whatsoever. All she could do was continue to attempt to gain his full trust. And wait for an opportunity to contact Ian again.

Not an optimum scenario.

Jane turned off the thoughts and focused on listening. Benson was no longer in sight. He expected her to be able to hear the car's engine start; to do that she had to focus.

What she didn't want to hear was gunfire…or sirens.

Or silence.

The seconds ticked off into minutes.

Still nothing.

Tension stiffed her muscles, urging her to check out the situation.

He wouldn't like it.

She could always turn around if she heard the engine start.

Moving slowly, noiselessly, she edged forward. Followed the same route he'd taken. When she got within sight of the gravel road that led past his house, she caught a glimpse of yellow crime scene tape flapping in the wind at the end of his driveway. If there were any cops around, they had pulled down the drive closer to the house. Which would make driving away less complicated.

Still no engine sound.

Not good.

She had backed into the overgrown drive. The trees and junglelike shrubbery had shielded her car from the road. Being seen on approach wasn't a concern…unless someone was lying in wait.

Reaching the edge of the clearing around the burned-out house, she leaned to the left to see past the orphaned chimney.

Damn.

Benson had his hands in the air. A man, wearing dark clothing as the shooters last night had, stood behind Benson, his weapon jammed into his spine.

As Jane watched, Benson dropped to his knees and laced his hands behind his head.

She couldn't be sure if the guy in black had already called his friends, or if he'd been left here alone and was to bring Benson to a rendezvous point if he showed up.

Jane clasped her weapon in both hands and started a cautious move toward the two men. The guy with the gun was preparing to secure Benson's hands. Looked like nylon cuffs. He slipped a cuff over Benson's right hand, twisted his arm down so that his hand was at the small of his back, then did the same with the other. Looped the final cuff and pulled tight.

At least now she knew this wasn't a dead-or-alive situation. Whoever had sent these men wanted Benson alive. Could have fooled her last night.

The guy in black kicked Benson in the side.

Bastard.

It was easy to be tough when one's opponent was restrained. The butt of the gun slammed into Benson's left jaw area. He toppled over.

Fury roared inside Jane. This guy was going to pay. *Jerk.*

While he was busy hauling Benson back to his feet, Jane moved in.

She jammed the muzzle of her weapon into the base of his skull. "Drop your weapon."

He froze.

"Drop your weapon *now*."

Jane braced for a reaction. Drew her right hand back, level with her shoulder.

He wasn't going to cooperate.

The thought had no more formed in her brain than he whirled toward her.

But she was ready for him.

She rammed the heel of her right hand into his nose.

He grabbed for his face.

She kicked him in the crotch with all her might.

He hit the ground.

"Now." She pressed the barrel of her weapon to his temple as he lay curled in a shuddering ball. "Let go of that weapon." Despite the painful attack, he'd kept a grip on that damned gun.

His fingers relaxed. She snatched the gun from his hand.

"You okay?" she asked Benson.

"Yeah."

He didn't look okay. His lip was bleeding and his left eye was already swelling.

While she patted down her prisoner with one hand, she kept the muzzle boring into his temple with the other. Maybe he had some more of those…

"That's what I'm looking for." She tugged a second pair of nylon cuffs from his pocket. "Facedown. Hands on the back of your head."

When he'd complied, she secured his hands the same way he had Benson's.

"Where're the others?" she demanded, ramming the muzzle even harder into his skull.

He snarled a particularly ugly curse at her.

"Answer the question," she repeated.

"He's not going to tell you anything." Benson had staggered over. "Let's just get out of here."

She stared up at him. "You want to leave him?"

"His friends will come back for him."

"We could take him with us," she offered.

Benson shook his head. "He'll be more trouble than he's worth."

"Guess this is your lucky day," she said to the guy. She pushed to her feet and started to turn away. Should have, but the ache in her side wouldn't let her. She kicked the hell out of him. He coughed. Gagged.

"Wait."

She turned to Benson.

"He's got the keys." He nodded toward the man on the ground. "In his left pocket."

Jane reached across him, tugged the keys from his pocket. He had a cell phone, too. She took that as well, turned it off and removed the battery before shoving it into her own pocket.

As soon as they were out of here, this guy would take off down the road. Some unsuspecting motorist might pick him up and end up dead.

Maybe she'd lessen the likelihood of him being picked up. She tugged off his boots. Then rolled him over and unfastened his trousers.

"What're you doing?" Benson demanded, his voice gruff with pain and impatience.

"Get in the car. I'll be right there."

She tugged the guy's trousers down his muscled legs and pulled them off his feet. "Good luck," she said as she stood. She tossed the pants aside. He'd never get them on with his hands secured behind his back.

Benson waited in the car for her.

She dropped behind the wheel and put the key in the ignition. "You want me to find something to cut you loose?"

"Just drive. We can do that later."

The swollen eye looked painful.

Ice would be good. She'd have to stop at a drive-through.

She nosed out onto the road, surveying both directions. Rolling slowly, she eased out onto the road in the direction of the main drag that led into Plano proper. Holding her breath and praying they wouldn't meet any other cars, particularly any official ones.

At the stop sign where Grissom Spring Road and the county road intersected, she asked, "Which way?"

"Left."

That surprised her but she did as he said.

"We're not going back to Plano. We're heading to Chicago."

Maybe he'd finally decided to give the Colby

Agency a chance. "You won't be sorry if you give my agency a shot at resolving—"

"I need a new ID. There's a guy in Chicago I can go to."

Since there was a possibility that the guy they'd left in the woods had put a tracking device on the car, Jane needed to pull over as soon as it was safe and give it a once-over.

And get Benson some ice, and cut him loose.

Her purse. She hadn't even thought of that. Glancing behind the console into the rear floor-board, she confirmed that it was there.

It was a miracle.

But the guys after them weren't petty thieves. They were here for Benson.

Since the guy back there in the woods had been preparing Benson for transport, it was safe to say he had a command performance with whomever he'd had trouble with four years ago.

He'd said he didn't trust the FBI. Evidently they had crossed him somehow.

A gas station and convenience store coming up on the right would work. She pulled in, parking on the side of the store. "I'll get you some ice."

He nodded once.

She grabbed her purse, tried to remember if she had any sort of over-the-counter pain reliever.

As soon as she stepped inside and smelled the coffee, she knew she had to have some. Coffee and something to fuel up on. She gathered drinks, snacks, two cups of ice, wipes, a pair of scissors and a tube of antibiotic ointment.

When she'd paid, she walked back to the car and cut Benson loose. With his hands free he immediately reached for a cup of the coffee.

"I have to check out something." She put her coffee in the console's cup holder and tossed the rest of the stuff she'd purchased into the backseat.

This would take a couple of minutes, but she knew the drill, knew what to look for.

Starting beneath the hood, she went over the car, methodically and carefully. This was far too important to blow it by rushing.

When she scooted out from under the car, Benson was crouched at the hood waiting for her. "What're you doing?"

"Making sure they didn't add a tracking device."

He made a face. "Now, there's something I hadn't thought about."

She got to her feet, swiped her palms together. "I think we're clean." She pointed to the stuff in the backseat. "There are some wipes back there and some ointment and ice if you want to clean up your face and try to slow that swelling."

He set his coffee on the roof of the car and climbed into the backseat.

"Be right back," she told him. "Bathroom."

Back inside the store, she walked straight to the back and locked herself in the bathroom. She stared at her reflection in the mirror. "Damn." She had herself a pretty good shiner. Not really any swelling, mainly bruising. She relieved herself, washed her face and hands and tried to detangle her hair. She should have grabbed the brush from her purse.

Usually she didn't really care. Especially at a time like this....

"Dumb, Jane," she said to her reflection.

Benson wasn't the slightest bit interested in her as a woman. He just wanted out of here.

That was when it hit her. She'd left him in the car. With the keys.

Chapter Eleven

Troy stared at the keys in the ignition.

He could drive away.

It would be better if he did.

Having Jane along would only risk her life again and again or get her killed.

Like Patsy.

When he'd confessed that he'd rescued the woman and kid, Patsy had asked about a reward. He knew the reason. His excuse for not pursuing a relationship had been money. He'd insisted that a woman—a family—deserved more than he could give. And that was true. But Patsy hadn't understood what he meant. She hadn't known his secrets. She had assumed he meant because he worked at the diner for a pittance.

She'd wanted to help him. So they could be together. And that desire had gotten her killed.

Another murder on his conscience.

Something else he would have to live with.

If his pathetic existence could be called living.

He should have been honest with Patsy and told her that he liked her for a friend, but nothing more. He hadn't wanted to hurt her…it seemed easier to give another kind of excuse.

Don't think about it right now…just drive away.

He stared at the keys again.

It was the right thing to do.

Jane had saved his ass back there.

He doubted he would have gotten this far without her. Leaving her stranded like this was no way to repay her.

Troy closed his eyes.

This was a mistake.

Another in a long line of big, bad choices.

Like trusting his uncle.

The driver's-side door opened and the decision was made.

Jane dropped behind the steering wheel. The look she sent in his direction told him she'd expected him to be gone when she got back out here.

"You didn't drive away." She started the engine.

"I thought about it."

When she'd pulled around the building and onto the road, she exhaled a big breath. "You did the right thing."

He didn't bother telling her that it had all boiled down to timing. If she'd been another four or five seconds, they wouldn't be having this conversation.

A few miles of silence elapsed. He spent most of that time watching her. She had herself a pretty good shiner, too. Her movements told him her ribs were sore. That made two of them. His lip was busted but good. And the swelling around his eye was going to be around a day or two. Maybe if he'd used the ice she'd gone to the trouble of getting…

Didn't matter.

As soon as he had an ID, he was getting a flight to D.C. It was time this ended. On his terms.

But to do that he needed money.

Damn it.

He'd forgotten the money.

"We have to go back."

She glanced at him. "You're kidding, right?"

He shook his head, grimaced at the pain that shot through his skull. "I have to get something from my mailbox."

"If anyone sees you—"

"That's where you come in."

She didn't argue, just slowed, then turned around.

He gave her directions for taking a roundabout way into town. One that took them closer to the Mail-Boxes-For-You where he got his mail. Which was mostly *current box-holder* stuff. But it served his purposes.

"Pull in the side lot," he instructed.

When she'd parked he dug the box key from his pocket. "Just get everything in the box."

She accepted the key, didn't ask any questions. This time she took the car keys with her.

Smart girl.

Three minutes later she returned with a stack of envelopes.

She shoved it at him as she climbed behind the wheel. "Are we ready to go now?"

"Head back to Chicago. I'll tell you where specifically to go when we're closer."

They could get a room outside Chicago. Then he could decide what to do with Jane.

He checked through the junk mail for the envelopes that contained his backup plan. Five envelopes addressed to him, each containing twenty-five hundred dollars. One also contained a key to a safe-deposit box at a Chicago bank. Once he'd started getting enough junk mail to keep the envelopes covered, he'd placed them in the mailbox. He checked the box from time to time, removing a few things, but careful to keep those five envelopes covered with a few other pieces of mail. He could access this box 24/7. And there was no record of what he had in there. The safe-deposit box held another twenty thousand dollars. Enough to facilitate a new start whenever necessary.

Part of him wanted to do just that. To never look back. Damn. When had he gotten so indecisive?

His gaze settled on Jane's profile once more. He'd passed up a couple of opportunities now to separate himself from her. He hoped he didn't live to regret the hesitation.

JANE DROVE. She didn't pursue additional attempts to persuade him to go to the Colby Agency with her. Let him think about all that had happened. How she'd helped him. And maybe he would decide to work with her.

Clearly those men weren't going to give up until they had accomplished their mission.

Her thoughts wandered to her mother. She had known Jane would be on assignment for a couple of days. But if she didn't get a call from her daughter soon, she would start to worry. With her heart condition, worry was the last thing she needed. When they got a room, Jane was making that call.

And one to Ian.

She'd turned off and removed the battery of the cell phone she'd taken from the guy back in the woods. With technology evolving every hour of every day, she wasn't going to risk the enemy using it as a tracking device.

She glanced at her passenger. "Was leaving your family behind difficult?" She kept her gaze on the road. The question was out of the blue, but they'd been silent long enough. She had to restart her fishing expedition at some point.

"No."

At least it was an answer.

"Sounds like you and your uncle weren't that close."

"We're not discussing my past."

Well, at least he was consistent.

"The landscape isn't that stimulating," she offered. "Conversation would be nice."

Instead of answering, he turned on the radio.

Great.

She drove another few miles, then turned the radio off. "What happened to your wife?"

He'd been married. That much she was sure of. Maybe he still was.

"She found someone who gave her what I couldn't."

Jane had to think a moment before responding to that announcement. "She cheated on you?" Might as well take it all the way.

"Yes."

The tall, silent types could sure as hell be a pain in the butt.

"Someone you knew?"

"What?"

She met his questioning gaze. "The other man. Someone you knew?"

"My uncle."

A bad, bad feeling welled in Jane's gut. "What did you do when you found out?"

"I wanted to kill him."

Please let that mean he hadn't.

He may be dangerous.

Funny thing was, he didn't feel dangerous…not like that anyway. Maybe dangerous to her sanity. She'd never met a man who made her glad to be a woman the way he did. Fate sure as hell had a warped sense of humor.

"But you didn't," she prodded when he didn't say more.

"No." He turned to stare out the passenger window. "I decided to do something worse."

Surely he didn't kill his wife.

"I thought about killing *her*, but I couldn't see myself living with the guilt."

He had a conscience. That was good.

"What could be worse than killing one or the other?"

"Sending his two sons to prison."

She sent him a sideways glance. "How did you do that?"

"That's one of those things we're not going to talk about, remember?"

Wow. He definitely knew how to get even.

He'd told her he had been a research scientist. "You were a part of the family business?"

Silence.

Ding-ding-ding. She'd nailed that one. His silence screamed *yes*.

"Your uncle and cousins were dirty," she went on, building a theory. "You'd suspected as much for a while, but didn't really want to believe it. Until your rage at your uncle blocked all other emotion."

"Two years."

She sent him another of those inquiring looks.

"That's how long I'd been in denial. I saw things. Questioned things. I think I knew all the time, but I didn't want it to be true."

"You turned him in. And the FBI put you in Witness Protection." Dear God, that was the answer. That was why he had no warm, fuzzy feelings for the bureau. They had failed him somehow.

"They set me up. That's what they did."

No wonder he despised the bureau. "Not all FBI agents are like that. The bad ones are the few."

"I knew as long as my name was somewhere in their system that I was vulnerable."

She could see his point. "So you took yourself out of the system."

"That's right."

"What made you decide to come to Plano?" It wasn't exactly one of those places that popped to mind when one considered places to spend the rest of one's life. At least not unless one had grown up there.

"It was close enough to Chicago that I could drive in on Sunday afternoons and enjoy the city."

"You like Chicago?" She studied him as long as she dared to take her attention off the road. He stared forward, his expression lost in the past.

"The last vacation my parents and I took as a family was to Chicago."

That very well could be one of the only good memories he had. "It's a great city."

More of that silence fell between them.

She'd learned more than she'd expected to. Whatever Ian's reasons for warning her that he might be dangerous were likely trumped-up stories to make him look like the bad guy his uncle and cousins were.

"What's the real reason you aren't married?" he asked, his question as random and abrupt as hers about what happened to his wife.

"Like I told you before—" she hated when people asked this question "—guys don't look at me and see wife material. I'm too…plain."

He laughed. "What are you talking about?"

"Plain." Why didn't he let this go? "You know, plain Jane? That's me. That's what the kids always called me."

"You are not plain."

They'd had this conversation before. "Was it money or kids your uncle gave your ex that you couldn't?"

"Both."

Wow. "You can't have kids?" She tried as long as she dared to read the dark expression on his face.

"I didn't want to have kids."

"You don't like kids?"

"I don't want to talk about this."

Okay. It wasn't like she really needed to know about that part of his past anyway.

"Did you have a home back in Silver Springs?"

"Yes."

"What happened to it?"

"Probably owned by the bank."

"That's a shame."

"Yeah, well. Life sucks that way sometimes."

She had to agree with that assessment. Ever since her father had died when she'd been twenty-two, she'd known that life was unfair. Otherwise a fine man like him would never have left this earth so early.

"Would you mind grabbing me one of those granola bars?" She wasn't really hungry, but eating always seemed to induce conversation. A few more key questions and she would have his story.

He reached for the bag in the back. Opened the wrapper and peeled it back before handing the snack to her. She munched on the crispy bar and considered that they were only about half an hour from downtown Chicago now. Maybe they needed to start looking for a room.

She had plenty of room at her place, but going there was out of the question. If the men had been watching her car, they would also be watching her place. Especially when it became clear that they weren't going to find him by any other means.

"When you disappeared, did someone help you?"

"I learned how to do what needed to be done on the Internet."

Wasn't that how everyone got their advice and answers these days?

"I was very careful. It would still be working if I hadn't gotten involved in that accident."

That had to be tough. He'd worked hard to build an existence after the harshest betrayal.

"But you did the right thing."

"Yeah."

He didn't sound so convinced, but that was more likely his weariness talking.

"We should get a room, take showers and grab some decent sleep. Being tired is the number-one reason humans make mistakes."

"Pick one," he said by way of agreement.

"Once we're settled, I need to make a couple of calls."

"We'll see."

That lingering distrust hadn't quite dissipated.

Maybe if she kept prompting him she would get to the real answers she needed.

He'd sent his two cousins to prison. His uncle was probably pissed beyond all reason, even now four years later. But none of that told her the charges. Had they been defrauding their own company?

"Does that look okay to you?" She indicated the chain motel up ahead.

"Fine."

Jane turned into the lot.

"Don't park too close to the entrance," he instructed.

She chose a spot several slots away from the main entrance and shut the engine off before turning to her passenger. "We can't exactly get the room in either of our names."

He passed a wad of cash to her. She took it, didn't bother asking where he'd gotten it. From one of the envelopes she'd taken from his mailbox most likely.

"They're going to want to see ID," Jane reminded him. "Cash they'll probably take, but we'll still need a driver's license."

"Use your persuasive skills." He reached out, touched her cheek where it was bruised. The feel of his fingers on her skin made her shiver. "Your husband is beating you. You had to get away but he can't know where you are."

This guy was good.

Good at making her feel things she hadn't felt before.

Good at escape scenarios.

And lying.

Chapter Twelve

Benson was right. The clerk, female and inordinately sympathetic, gave Jane a room with no ID and no credit card. Just cash.

She could take a moment to call Ian. Benson wouldn't dare come looking for her. But she couldn't use the shooter's cell phone.

Moving back to the counter, Jane leaned forward. "Is it possible for me to use a phone?"

The clerk glanced around. "Sure." She indicated the phone on the desk. "Just dial eight for an outside line."

Jane chewed her lower lip. "I was hoping to use one that wouldn't give away my exact location."

"Oh." The clerk blinked, thought about the request for a moment. "You could use my cell."

Jane breathed a big sigh. "That'd be great." She

smiled, ordered her lips to tremble. "I'd really appreciate it."

"Not a problem." The clerk glanced around the lobby to ensure that no one was waiting for her attention. "Give me a minute."

She moved to the other end of the counter and dug around underneath. When she returned to where Jane waited she passed the cell across the counter.

"Thanks." Jane moved away from the front desk. She quickly entered Ian's number. Scanned the front entrance for any sign of Benson.

"Michaels."

"It's Jane. I can't talk long."

"Give me your location."

"Good Night Inn. About twelve miles west of downtown. Benson has found some contact here who can provide him with a new identity. At least a temporary one. He's keeping the details to himself."

"His name is Trace Beckman," Ian informed her. "Four years ago he rolled over on his two cousins, Bradley and Kenneth Beckman."

"Are you talking about Beckman Technology?" She remembered seeing something about it in the news. The company was accused of selling military technology to an organization with suspected terrorist ties.

"That's the one."

"Holy cow." Well, he'd said he was a research scientist.

"Shortly before the trial started his soon-to-be ex-wife was murdered. The case remains unsolved."

"Benson or Beckman was a suspect?"

"Yes. The details get blurry after that. He may have cut a deal considering his testimony was the sole way to convict his cousins."

"I get the feeling he believes the feds double-crossed him when it came to the Witness Protection bit."

"His file reads as if protection was never offered, but that would be extraordinarily unusual."

"Anything else?"

"Watch your step. We have the elder Beckman under surveillance. My contact at the bureau believes the uncle is the one to watch in this."

"Thanks, Ian." Jane surveyed the entrance once more. "I'll be in touch. If it's essential that you contact me, call Benson's cell." She rattled off the number she'd heard him give his contact.

Jane returned the cell phone to the clerk. "Thanks."

The clerk nodded. "Take care of yourself. You know," she said when Jane would have walked away, "there are people who can help with abusive spouses."

Jane patiently waited through the woman's suggestions, thanked her, then hustled out to the car. Benson—Beckman—was likely getting antsy by now.

"The room's around back." She slid behind the wheel. "Ground floor."

"Took you long enough."

Jane backed out of the parking slot. "Persuasion takes time, Benson. You gotta make your story real."

He made a noncommittal sound, but didn't take his eyes off her as she drove around to the back of the building.

Suspicious. Another step back on the matter of trust.

At the room Benson took the key from her and opened the door. A shower was the first order of business. She hoped he would be as much of a gentleman about who went first as he had been about holding the door.

Two double beds. She breezed through the room, tossed her purse and keys onto one of the beds. It smelled fairly clean. Bathroom looked clean. This would be a pleasant change after sleeping on that filthy floor last night.

"You want to shower first?"

She turned to him. "Thanks. I'll definitely take you up on that one."

"I'll order some food."

"Awesome." She was starved. Jane headed for

the bathroom but hesitated. "When are you calling your contact?"

"Tonight." He placed his weapon on the night table between the beds. "We'll make arrangements to meet. He only conducts business in person."

She backed toward the bathroom door. "Five minutes. That's all I need."

Part of her hated to go into that room and close the door. He could leave. Just take off and disappear. But he'd had opportunities to do that already.

Still, she stalled in the doorway and stared longingly at the bed where she'd left her keys.

Even if she took the keys into the bathroom with her, if he was going, he would find a way.

Trust.

She couldn't expect it from him if she didn't show the same.

Put your money where your mouth is, girl. She stepped fully into the bathroom and closed the door behind her. A twist of the faucet handle got the water flowing from the showerhead. After kicking off her shoes, she peeled off her socks and blouse, then wiggled out of her slacks. She had no choice but to put those clothes back on. If she washed them in the tub, chances were they wouldn't dry overnight. Not to mention that would leave her naked.

She'd just have to deal with soiled clothes.

The panties and bra were another story. She climbed into the shower wearing both. When she had savored the hot water flowing over her body long enough to feel relaxed, she dragged off the wet panties and unhooked the soggy bra. Using the tiny soap bar, she washed both. Rinsed and squeezed her undies thoroughly, then hung them over the shower curtain rod. Next she smoothed the soap over her skin. Her ribs were still sore, as was her cheek. But the hot water went a hell of a long way in making her feel so, so much better.

And her hair. God, if she weren't so tired she could massage her scalp and hair all night.

But she'd promised Benson five minutes.

She was relatively certain she'd used up that allotment several minutes ago.

Shutting off the water, she shoved the curtain aside, stepped out and grabbed the towel. Scrubbing her hair with the towel, she reached out with her free hand and swiped the steam from the mirror. The bruise on her cheek was not so bad. More in her hairline than on her face.

He'd said she was attractive. Cute. But she wasn't. She was plain. Ordinary. Anyone could see that. He was the one who was attractive.

What kind of woman would push away a guy

who looked like that? Not that looks were everything. Clearly he was a good guy. He'd risked his life to rescue a stranger and her son. Why hadn't his wife appreciated his compassion?

He'd saved Jane's butt that night at his house, when he could certainly have run…escaped his pursuers much easier without her in tow.

Had she thanked him for that?

She had returned the favor today…but her mother would say that wasn't an actual thank-you, it was just doing the right thing.

Quickly pulling on her slacks and blouse, she grabbed the towel and dried her hair a little more. Then she cleaned up her mess and slid her undies to one side. There really wasn't any place to put them where he wouldn't see. Big deal. They were adults. She imagined he'd seen plenty, probably far more frilly and feminine than her serviceable bikini briefs.

"Whatever." She opened the door and shivered when the cool, conditioned air rushed over her. "It's all yours."

She stopped a few feet from the door. The room was empty.

Her gaze swung to the bed where she'd left the keys.

The keys were gone.

Jane rushed to the door. Locked. She twisted the lock and wrenched open the door.

The car was gone.

He was gone.

TROY SAT in the parking lot of the supercenter. All he had to do was make the call, get a rendezvous location and go.

He could get his ID and be out of here well before dark. That would be the easiest route to go.

But would that really end this thing?

Only until he was outed again.

He would have to watch his every move, avoid getting close to anyone, for the rest of his life.

Life. That was no life.

What was he doing?

Troy stared at a woman climbing out of a minivan a few parking spaces away. She shoved the sliding door open and helped her kids out. The three strolled across the parking lot to the store's entrance.

Normal.

It had been so long since he'd had anything remotely normal in his life….

He shifted his gaze to the cell phone on the console.

If he'd made the call already, he could get what he needed and be headed out of here.

Why hesitate?

He thought of the waitress…his friend…Patsy. His actions had caused her death.

No matter how he analyzed it, the answer was the same. His being in Plano—his hiding out—caused her to lose her life.

How did two rights make a wrong?

He'd cooperated with the FBI and stopped the travesty his own family had wielded. He'd given up his life in order to do that.

Then just when he'd figured he would spend the rest of his life slinging hash…he'd been faced with another choice. Protect himself or save two lives. Or, at least, attempt to.

Jane insisted that the Colby Agency could help him. How the hell could some PI firm fix this mess when the bureau hadn't been able to?

The answer was simple, they couldn't.

He just wanted to believe this woman who'd barged into his life.

When had he gotten so stupid?

Maybe he was just tired.

Tired of fighting this battle of wills. The world would have been a better place if the old bastard had died long ago.

But he just kept on breathing.

Fury twisted in Troy's gut.

He reached for the cell phone.

JANE PACED back and forth in the room. She should call Ian.

But there was nothing he could do.

If Benson was gone, he had too much of a head start to track him down. The rental would show up eventually. But he would be long gone.

She didn't know the name of the contact he'd intended to meet. The Colby Agency could run the names of all known identity counterfeiters in the area…but that would take time.

Jane stopped. She was wasting time. Buying time, actually.

Part of her wanted to believe that Benson would come back. That he'd gone to meet his contact and would return to the room after he'd taken care of business.

Forty-five minutes and counting.

He wasn't coming back.

She stalked over to the night table and picked up the phone.

The door opened, rammed against the security chain.

"It's me."

Relief rushed through her limbs.

She stamped over to the door and released the chain, swung the door open. "Where the hell have you been?"

He pushed past her, his arms loaded with bags.

She slammed the door and locked it. *Calm down.* Making a scene wasn't going to get her any answers.

"I picked up some things we needed."

"What things?"

"Clothes. Food."

"You said you were going to order food."

"No room service." He picked through the bags, pulled out a T-shirt and jeans. "I wasn't in the mood for pizza." He tossed one of the bags across the bed toward her. "I hope I got the sizes right."

She peeked into the bag. Jeans. T-shirt. Even underwear. Pink, frilly, very feminine. Exactly what she wouldn't buy. There was also deodorant, toothpaste and a brush.

"Thanks." The word was chock-full of frustration.

He settled his gaze on hers. "I guess I should've left you a note."

"You think?" She grabbed her bag of goodies and stomped to the bathroom.

Her body heated the instant the satin panties settled against her skin. She looked down at herself. Flat stomach. Toned legs. She had the body for wearing stuff like this but she never did. Why bother?

Did he see her this way?

Her face flushed at the thought.

"Ridiculous." She wrapped the bra around her

torso and fastened it. The satin cupped her breasts as if he measured them with his own hands. Another shiver rippled through her. The T-shirt was a perfect fit. Same with the jeans. Maybe he'd assessed her physically more closely than she'd realized.

She put the deodorant and toothbrush to use. Her tongue slid across her teeth. Felt good to have clean teeth. And fresh undies.

Grabbing her dirty clothes, she exited the bathroom and shoved them into the trash can. She was fairly certain they were beyond help.

"Sandwich?"

He'd already made himself a bologna sandwich and was working on a second.

"Sure." She plopped down on the bed where she'd tossed her purse.

He passed her a cold drink, then the sandwich. "You're angry."

"You should have told me." She bit into the sandwich.

"I should've."

She chewed, swallowed. "Why didn't you?"

His gaze locked with hers. "I was going to call my contact. Pick up the ID and go."

Jane tore off another bite of the sandwich and chewed it methodically. "Why didn't you?"

"I don't know."

There was something different about him. A resignation she hadn't seen before.

"Thanks for the clothes." She pulled at the T-shirt. "I'll pay you back."

His gaze flicked from hers to her breasts.

"Don't worry about it." He took a long swallow of his soda.

She licked her lips hungrily. Told herself the abrupt glimmer of desire had nothing to do with watching him.

He set the can aside. "Tell me about this agency you work for."

Anticipation quickened her pulse. "We find the truth. Help every client who comes through the door."

"What levels of crime is your agency prepared to tackle?"

Jane laughed. "You name it. The Colby Agency has *tackled* it all. Our investigators come from all walks of life. Military. Bureau. The medical field." She shrugged. "Every level of expertise. No case is too small or too large."

"The other investigators—" he pulled his legs up onto the bed, propped against the headboard "— they're like you? Well trained? Focused?"

"They're the best. The very best." She considered the man. He'd just given her an offhanded compliment. "We can help you. Whatever your story, the Colby Agency can find the answers you need." Telling him she knew his story might not go over so well. It would be better if he made the decision to tell her.

"This contact," he said, his attention on the television screen across the room, "he can provide me with a new identity. For the right price, he can also provide a permanent escape."

"Permanent?" She had an inkling what he meant. Faking his death.

"Fiery car crash. Boating accident. There are several choices."

"Can he provide the necessary body as well?" If so, he was a hell of a contact.

Benson nodded. "He claims he has influence at a local funeral home and can make the whole thing quite convincing."

"Sounds like a real stand-up guy."

He stared at his hands then. As if there was something about them he didn't like…or that he'd done something with them that he wished he hadn't.

His ex-wife had been murdered.

Could this man have committed murder?

Jane didn't want to think so…but he'd based his entire existence these past four years on lies and had been successful.

Not exactly a good foundation for honesty.

"So what happens next?"

He turned to her. "I'm leaning toward dying."

Chapter Thirteen

Something was wrong.

The feeling was overwhelming. Victoria surveyed the street in front of her home as Lucas guided their car into the drive.

"Where is Simon's car?" She turned to Lucas as he parked. "He should be here with Merri and Jamie." Fear sent her heart into a faster rhythm.

"Stay put while I check things out."

Before she could argue, Lucas had emerged from the car and started up the walk to the front door.

Victoria slipped her cell phone from her purse and entered Merri's number. Ring after ring echoed in her ear before the call went to voice mail.

"This isn't right." Victoria pushed open her door and got out. She hurried up the walk.

Lucas met her at the door. "There's no one here." His tone was grave. "Simon's cell goes straight to voice mail."

Dear God.

Victoria shook her head. This couldn't be happening. They had taken every precaution.

She pushed past Lucas, moved from room to room inside her home.

Lucas was on the phone. She could hear him asking questions. The fear that had set her heart to racing tightened around her chest and squeezed.

Please, please, don't let Barker have gotten to Jamie.

The entire house looked just as Victoria had left it that afternoon. She'd picked Jamie up from school and brought her here. Then she'd returned to the office for a meeting with those of her staff working on finding Barker. Merri and Simon had been here with Jamie.

This couldn't be.

Victoria stalled in the center of her living room.

It couldn't be happening again.

The cell phone slipped from her fingers, clattered on the floor.

"Victoria."

She turned to Lucas.

"They're at the office. We must have just

missed them. Jamie is safe. She's with Ian and the others."

The relief buckled Victoria's knees.

Lucas was suddenly next to her. "It's all right, darling." His strong arms went around her. "We're going to stop him. One way or another."

The Colby Agency, 7:45 p.m.

VICTORIA RUSHED off the elevator into the lobby. Lucas remained close behind her.

"See what Merri got me!" Holding a pretty pink purse, Jamie rushed to her grandmother. "There's even a mirror." She opened the little purse and showed Victoria the small attached mirror.

"It's beautiful." Victoria hugged the child close, her emotions so close to the surface that it took every ounce of strength she possessed to hold them back.

"Jamie."

The child pulled away from her grandmother and turned to Merri.

"Let's go to Ms. Mildred's office and get the picture you drew Lucas."

With a nod to Victoria, Merri took Jamie's hand in hers and headed to Mildred's office.

"What happened?" Victoria directed the question to Ian and Simon. "Jamie should never have been taken from the house without my explicit authorization."

"We don't know yet how Barker managed to tap in to our secure lines," Ian explained, "but he did."

"Apparently, he recorded several of our communications and used those to create a new call." Simon picked up the details from there.

"What call?" Lucas asked.

Victoria held her breath. The thought that this man could reach into their most secure communications sent a chill straight to her bones.

"Merri received a voice mail directing her to bring Jamie back here. The originating number was yours, Victoria, or appeared to be. Merri brought the call to my attention since she thought it was strange. But the voice was yours so we complied with the request."

"From this point on," Lucas recommended, "we should verify all directives."

"I attempted to verify the directive," Simon clarified. "Each time I called your cell or Victoria's, the calls went straight to voice mail."

Victoria shook her head. "I didn't receive a call."

"Nor did I," Lucas seconded.

"He's in our system," Ian surmised. "Controlling where the calls go. I've directed Ted Tallant and Kendra Todd to find the security breach and take the necessary actions to resolve the situation."

Kendra and Ted were two of the agency's top research analysts. With those two on the task, the situation would be under control soon.

"He's toying with us," Lucas said, the fury in his tone unmistakable. "He wanted us to know that he can get to Jamie despite our security measures."

Victoria wished Jim and Tasha were here already. "Until this situation is resolved," Victoria announced, her own fury burning past the more fragile emotions, "all communications will be face-to-face."

It was a drastic measure, but an essential one.

"I agree," Ian confirmed. "We'll have an all-hands meeting tomorrow morning and ensure that everyone understands that there will be no exceptions."

"I'll put the word out about the meeting," Simon volunteered. "And check up on Ted and Kendra's progress."

"I'd like to have an update as soon as possible," Victoria told him before he headed to his office.

"How close are your specialists to locating this man?" Ian asked Lucas.

"They're getting close," Victoria's husband relayed, "but obviously not close enough."

Or fast enough, Victoria considered. But Clayton Barker was a man as highly trained as those specialists seeking him. He would not make it easy.

"Let's add another layer of security to Jamie,"

Victoria said to her second in command. "Just in case."

"I'll see to it," Ian agreed.

"Have we heard anything else from Jane?" Victoria had the presence of mind to ask. This entire ordeal had shaken her as nothing else ever had—not in more than two decades.

"Jane and Mr. Beckman—aka Troy Benson—are safe in a motel outside Chicago for the night. Jane hopes to convince Mr. Beckman to allow the Colby Agency to help him. She believes she's having some level of success."

"Excellent." Victoria had every confidence that Jane would accomplish her goal.

The telephone on the receptionist's desk rang.

All attention zeroed in on the single button flashing in warning that a call was coming in.

Ian moved to the desk and picked up the receiver. "The Colby Agency."

As he listened to the caller, Ian's gaze collided with Victoria's. "I'll put you on speaker," he said to the caller.

Ian pressed the necessary buttons and laid the receiver back in its cradle. "Go head, Barker, you're on speaker. Both Victoria and Lucas are standing by."

"Lucas Camp," the loathsome voice said, "don't

put too much stock in your team's skills. They're not nearly as good as you think they are."

"Time will tell," Lucas countered.

"What do you want, Barker?" Victoria demanded. Her blood started to boil. She would love to be the one to put a bullet through this bastard's brain. Anyone who would use a child like this didn't deserve to keep breathing.

"I thought I'd already made that clear," he said with a laugh. "Ten million, Victoria, not one cent less. Your time is running out. Surely my little exercise this evening proved beyond a shadow of a doubt that I can get to that sweet little granddaughter of yours any time I want to."

The rage exploded in Victoria's chest. "And yet you continue to play these meaningless games. Perhaps you can't get as close as you'd like. Surely you don't believe these scare tactics will get you what you want."

Laughter boomed from the speaker. "Truly, Victoria, you are one of a kind. Believe what you will, but I'm quite certain my so-called scare tactics worked extraordinarily well. After all, you were scared, were you not?"

"I have no desire to waste any more of my time. Goodbye, Mr. Barker," Victoria announced.

Ian hit the proper button, severing the connection.

Victoria looked from Ian to Lucas. "Whatever it takes, gentlemen, I want this man taken down."

He deserved to be with his old friend Leberman—in hell.

Chapter Fourteen

Chicago's Warehouse District, 9:00 p.m.

"You're certain this is what you want to do."

She still believed that allowing the Colby Agency to take care of this situation would be in his best interest. Troy couldn't take the risk that they would fail.

He had to do this the only way he knew for certain would work.

He had to die…again. From that point, he could make decisions about what to do regarding his uncle.

Four years ago when he'd realized going into Witness Protection was nothing more than a death sentence, he'd taken matters into his own hands. The bureau had actually made it quite easy. They'd set him up with a supposedly new and protected identity down in Florida. He'd planned his death to the last detail. There had even been a couple of witnesses. He'd gone over the side of the boat and rescuers hadn't been able to find him. The waters had been searched for days with no luck. The witnesses had reported that he'd gotten far too drunk…and everyone had fallen for it. Even the bureau.

Evidently his uncle had been smarter than Troy had presumed. He'd kept an eye out for any sign of his nephew. His bureau contacts had likely done the same.

He would have to be more careful this time. They would know if he'd tried it once, he might try it again. Even if they were convinced, the chances of his uncle giving up completely were slim.

If Troy were lucky the old bastard would die before he discovered Troy's location the next time.

That little voice that he couldn't keep completely at bay railed at him. Reminded him that what he was doing was the easy way out. He exiled the voice, couldn't think beyond the moment.

Jane was still waiting for an answer. "It's the only way."

"For the record, I think you're making a mistake."

"Maybe."

A dark sedan rolled to a stop on the long stretch of alleyway that backed up to the row of warehouses.

"Is that him?"

"That's him." Troy reached for the door.

"I'm going with you."

"That's not a good idea."

Jane got out of the car anyway. Not much he could do about her hardheadedness since the guy in the other vehicle had no doubt seen her.

Troy wanted to be angry but somehow he couldn't. He'd told this woman he was moving forward with his own plan and still she insisted on hanging in with him for the duration. What was that about?

She couldn't possibly care whether he lived or died.

Surely she didn't believe she could still talk him into meeting with Norcross for the reward.

Jane Sutton baffled him.

As they approached the dark sedan the driver's window powered down. "Who's the woman?" The driver looked from Troy to Jane and back.

"A friend."

The man behind the wheel stared at Jane for a long moment, then turned his attention back to Troy. "Get in." He flicked a glance at Jane. "Only you."

She opened her mouth to argue, but Troy shot her a look and she snapped it closed.

He opened the car door closest to him and

climbed into the backseat. A man sat on the other side of the seat, fiftyish, gleaming bald head and fiercely intent eyes. The elegant suit he wore didn't fit with the deadly expression that appeared permanently etched across his face.

"Five thousand now," the man said, "five more after the accident."

Troy didn't want to have second thoughts. He wanted to do what he had to do. To get this done. For years he'd thought it didn't really matter if he lived or died, but he wasn't going to make it easy for his scumbag uncle. Suddenly his future felt very important.

"The body," Troy inquired, needing to be certain, "this is someone who's already dead, right?"

The man nodded. "As I told you before, I have my sources. I don't deal in murder, Mr. Benson. Only in escapes."

Okay, he should stop beating around the bush. Troy withdrew the envelope containing the money. "Five thousand." He passed it to the man.

"I'll need your wallet."

"Yeah, of course." His personal effects would be discovered near the charred remains. He fished the wallet from his pocket and passed it to the man.

"The police report will indicate you were robbed. The perp hit you with his vehicle. Your skull, the entire facial area will have been crushed, making identification next to impossible. There won't be any fingerprints since the perp opted to douse you in charcoal starter and light a match."

"All that won't garner suspicion?" Sounded like a hell of a lot of trouble to go through just to empty a man's wallet.

He lifted a skeptical brow. "Strange things happen in this city all the time."

"So, what do I do now?"

The man smirked. "If I were you, I'd stay out of sight until you get a call from me."

Troy nodded, then reached for the door.

"What about her?"

He looked back at the man who'd spoken. "What about her?"

"A smart man doesn't leave loose ends." He tucked the envelope of money into his jacket pocket. "I'd hate to see you waste your money."

Troy ignored his comment and got out of the car. He walked over to where Jane waited by the rental. The dark sedan rolled away. Troy didn't like that guy.

What the hell was he doing dealing with people like that? He should've taken off already, gotten as far from here as possible.

And spent the rest of his life moving from place to place?

Professional help was necessary.

He had to do this right.

"So, it's done?"

His attention shifted to Jane. "It's done."

"What now?"

"I wait for his call."

"You're making a mistake." She didn't wait for him to respond, she settled behind the wheel of her rented car and waited for him to climb in.

Troy didn't move for a moment. He stood there, staring at nothing at all and wondering how the hell this had happened to him. Why hadn't he done something sooner? Probably for the same reason he hadn't noticed his wife cheating on him.

Too focused on his work.

Not paying attention.

What he should have done four years ago was stayed until his uncle was brought to his knees. Troy would likely have been dead before the goal was accomplished. But at least he would have tried.

Instead, he walked away. Away from his work, his entire life.

Now he was doing it all over again. Only this time he had nothing to lose.

He'd already lost all that mattered to him.

The Good Night Inn, 10:40 p.m.

JANE PACED the room. She'd spent the last twenty minutes attempting to persuade Benson to let the Colby Agency help. But he wasn't listening.

Adding to her tension was the fact that she had allowed so much time to get away without touching base with her mother. She felt tempted to call her now. But if there was any chance that Beckman's people were listening in on her mother's phone line, that move could put her mother in danger and give them Benson's location.

A chirp signaled Benson had a call on his cell.

She turned toward where he sat on the bed as he took the call.

"Benson."

Had to be his contact. Jane understood that he thought he was doing the only thing he could, but that didn't make her feel any better about the choice he was making.

"I understand." He closed the phone and tossed it onto the bed. "Midnight." His gaze connected with Jane's as he pushed to his feet. "I should get ready."

How could such an elaborate plan be ready at midnight? "Seems a little soon to pull together such an involved scheme."

He glanced over his shoulder. "Maybe the guy's just good."

"And maybe he's only after your money and you'll end up dead for real." The more she thought about this, the less she liked it.

"Maybe." He tossed his few personal items, toothbrush, the other change of clothes he'd bought, into a bag.

"Look." She stalked over to him. "I know you don't trust anybody. I understand the FBI screwed you over. But there's another option here if you'll just listen to what I've been trying to tell you."

He picked up the bag and took it over to the door and set it on the floor. "I heard every word you've said. And I appreciate your faith in your employer." He turned to her. "But as long as they know I'm alive, people are going to get hurt. This is the best option." He searched her eyes a moment. "If you knew my uncle, you'd know it's the only option."

Jane shook her head. Her instincts were humming. "Here's the deal." This could go either way. She'd been wrestling with this for hours. "I do know who your uncle is. Who you are."

His posture went rigid.

"Trace Beckman. Dr. Trace Beckman."

"How long have you known?"

"Since we checked in." She braced for his

reaction. "I had the clerk eating out of my hand. She let me use her cell phone. I called the agency."

"How did they learn my identity?"

This was where things would get sticky. "From your prints."

His nostrils flared. "My prints?"

"Yeah. From the coleslaw order."

Realization dawned on his face. "Then you're the one responsible for my uncle learning my whereabouts. Not Patsy."

She shook her head. "No. Remember, I didn't get your prints till four-thirty or so. Even if my agency ran them immediately, your uncle wouldn't have had time to dispatch his people that quickly. Patsy's journalist friend is how he found out."

Benson gave her that silent treatment he was so good at for a minute or more. "Doesn't matter now." He walked over to the window and peeked out around the curtains.

"I think you're making a mistake." She moved up next to him. "This contact of yours got this thing pulled together way too fast. This isn't going to work out the way you think."

"I guess you're an expert." He didn't look at her as he spoke.

"A better one than you."

He did look at her then. "How so? I'm the one

who set up a new identity and carried it off for four years—without any help."

"And, if you're lucky, maybe you'll have the chance again. The truth of the matter is, you'll have to do it again and again. Every time he finds you, you'll have to start over."

"Until he's dead."

She turned to him. "You planning on killing him? Maybe that would be the easiest way out of this. Don't kill yourself. Kill him."

He shifted his attention back to the darkness beyond the window. The parking lot was mostly empty. "Don't think I haven't thought about it."

"Are you a killer, Trace?"

He blinked.

"Did you kill your ex-wife? Old man Beckman says you did, but the feds don't think so."

His gaze narrowed. "How do you know what the feds think?"

"I told you, the Colby Agency has contacts. Good contacts. They can fix this."

"They can't fix this. It won't stop until he's dead."

"So your uncle was removed enough from the dirty business that when your cousins took the fall, he was immune?"

"That's right."

"Who's been doing his dirty work since your

cousins were imprisoned?" There had to be someone else. "That person might be approachable."

"There's no way to know if he's still involved with his old friends. He made several fortunes in a very short time. He got his share and his two sons' as well. I'm the only one who can prove what he did. Getting rid of me is just housekeeping."

"And maybe a little vengeance."

"Maybe."

"Wait. Did you say you're the only one who can prove what he did?"

His gaze locked with hers. "That's right."

"Then why didn't the bureau take him down when they took his two sons down?"

"There was a key element missing in the evidence I'd amassed."

"Are you saying you have this key element now?" Jane didn't see how that was possible.

"When he killed…Gwen, I didn't care anymore. I was finished. Just before I disappeared I got something in the mail from her. Something she'd sent before…he killed her. But it was too late to make a difference at the time. Or maybe I just wanted to think that because I didn't care anymore."

"The missing evidence you needed," Jane guessed.

He shook his head. "She didn't have access to that, but she had set up monitoring devices all over the house. She had an audio recording of a telephone conversation. He was giving an order that explicitly incriminates him."

What the hell? "Why haven't you turned this over to the authorities?"

He laughed. "I don't trust the bureau anymore, Jane." He glared at her. "Don't you get that? For all I know my uncle could have made some sort of deal with them. I'm not going down that path again."

She nodded. "I see. You're scared. Scared and desperate."

He whirled on her. "Scared?" He leaned closer. "You think I'm scared?"

"Aren't you?" Jane held her ground. She needed him to get mad. To regain his determination. He'd given up and that was forcing him down the wrong path.

"Fear is not what drives me, Ms. Sutton. But I know when I'm outdone. I can't fight the bureau. If I attempt to prove what they've done, they'll just turn this whole thing around on me and then I'll end up in prison with my two favorite cousins."

"My agency found no indication from the bureau that you've ever been a suspect in your cousins' criminal activities."

"But that might change if the man inside the bureau who cut him a deal feels threatened."

The stare-off continued, but Jane couldn't argue with his reasoning. But she could offer a plan B.

"Then we don't go through the bureau. We trap your uncle into a confession. The Colby Agency can help make it happen. Ian Michaels and Simon Ruhl have contacts in the bureau who can be trusted." She held her breath, hoped like hell he would trust her.

He turned back to the window. "I already have a plan. This will be over soon."

Damn it! "But is that really the way you want it to end?" *Come on, Jane! Say the right thing.* "Obviously Gwen had second thoughts before she died."

A muscle ticked in his jaw.

"She tried to help you. Maybe that's why she's dead."

Another of those furious glares pointed in her direction.

"If you just let him get away with it, she died for nothing."

She saw the indecision…saw the flicker of vengeance her words elicited.

Then he turned away. "I have to go soon."

Then she went for broke. "Funny."

"What's funny?" He reached for his bag.

"The idea that all this time I thought you were a hero. I guess I was wrong."

Chapter Fifteen

He had to go.

Troy closed his eyes and tried to block the hope that her words generated.

It was too late to salvage his life. Too late to fix what was over and done.

Memories of his ex-wife surfaced, muddying his already muddled thoughts. She'd cheated on him, gone for the money. He'd thought she was a heartless bitch. But she'd had a conscience after all.

His fingers tightened on his bag. He should go. Forget all of this.

He turned to Jane. "I never claimed to be a hero. Just a guy with unfortunate timing."

Seriously unfortunate timing.

"Fine." She grabbed her purse and her keys. "I'll

drop you off." She reached for the door. "It's the least I can do."

"I still have time to call for a taxi. At this hour there shouldn't be a problem."

"Don't be ridiculous." She walked out the door.

Troy hesitated. He could just make the call and ignore her waiting in the car.

What the hell?

He gave up and got in the passenger seat.

The rendezvous was near the pier. Troy would be taken to a safekeeping location until the job was done. While he was there his hair color would be changed and he would be fitted with colored contacts. He would be provided with video proof of the accident and at that time he would pay the remainder of his fee. The final service provided was being dropped at a point of public transportation. Bus, train, plane, whatever his choice.

"If you would trust me with this evidence you have," Jane offered, "I could see what Ian and Simon can do without your participation."

"Why are you doing this?" Troy stared at her profile. He couldn't figure this woman out. "It's not like you're going to be able to give your client what he wants. Why not call it a day and go home?"

For once she was the silent one.

She kept quiet so long he had begun to think she wasn't going to respond to him at all when she finally answered.

"You deserve your life back."

The words hit him like a tidal wave, washed over and over his senses. "Why would you care?"

She shook her head. "I don't know. Maybe I'm crazy. But I guess I believe in the good guy winning. You're the good guy in this. You should win."

Was this woman for real?

This was not the time for him to get all sentimental. It wasn't the time to start believing in happily-ever-afters, either.

"This is one of those times," he countered, "that you should just pretend the last couple of days didn't happen. The life you're trying to save isn't worth the effort."

"Now you're just feeling sorry for yourself." She slowed for a turn.

Feeling sorry for himself? Was she trying to pick a fight with him? "Guilty as charged. See, I told you I'm not worth the trouble."

"What do you care if I pursue the truth about your uncle? You'll be gone anyway. Maybe you'll catch the headlines or see him on the news. Justice is served, better late than never."

If it were only that easy. "I'll pass. The fact that

he can't get his hands on me will be enough punishment to satisfy me."

He'd just learned something new about Jane Sutton. She didn't like to lose.

"I really hate this," she snapped.

He wasn't about to take that bait.

"You tough guys." She shook her head. "You love to act so macho and like you're not afraid of anything, but then when it comes to true commitment, you're ready to cut and run."

Oh yeah. She was seriously trying to get a reaction.

"I'm not changing my mind."

"Fine."

"You said that already."

Then there was more of that silence. For blocks and blocks.

By the time they reached the parking area of the agreed-upon location near the pier, he was ready to kick something.

She turned off the ignition. "I guess this is it."

Headlights flashed on, then off across the parking lot. His contact was here.

"You'll go home from here?" Dumb question but it was the first one to come to mind.

"Yeah. My mom's probably worried."

Troy smiled.

"You think it's funny because a woman my age is so close to her mom?"

"No." He was tired. Too tired to figure out how to end this *thing*. "I think it's sweet."

"Get out of the car, Benson."

"Yeah." He opened the door and got out, reached into the backseat for his bag.

He glanced at her, she kept her attention forward. *Just go, Troy.*

He closed the door and took a couple of steps in the direction of the sedan waiting across the parking lot. But he stalled. Decided there was one thing he had to do. He rounded the hood and opened the driver's-side door.

Jane glared up at him. "What?"

"Get out of the car."

She didn't argue, released her seat belt and got out. She folded her arms over her chest and lifted her chin defiantly.

If he took a second to think about it, he would probably realize what a stupid move this was.

But he didn't think about it. He dropped his bag and kissed her.

Kissed her long and deep.

She leaned into him and his body reacted.

How long had it been since he'd kissed anyone like this?

He didn't know…didn't care.

She tasted warm and soft…sweet. Just like he'd known she would.

His arms went around her, pulling her closer, tucking her hips against his. She made the sweetest sound.

But he had to go….

He drew his lips from hers, but couldn't bear to break the connection completely. His arms stayed snugly around her, his forehead pressed against hers.

"You make me wish things were different." He had to be out of his mind to say those words.

"The choice is yours." She raised her lips to his and started that spinning whirlwind of sensations all over again.

Her arms went around his neck, her breasts flattened against his chest. Need detonated in his body.

She pushed him back. "Look me up sometime if you change your mind." She climbed back into the car. "You know where I'll be."

The door closed. The thud echoed in his brain.

He was doing the right thing.

It was the only way.

He picked up his bag and started walking toward the escape that would, if he were damned lucky, end all this. Jane Sutton would be a lot better off without his problems in her life.

He was damaged goods.

The waiting sedan's rear driver's-side door opened and his contact emerged.

Troy's cell phone chirped.

His contact was here.

No one else had his number.

He didn't recognize the caller.

He stalled, opened the phone. "Benson."

"Do you know how long it took to track down this number?"

Dread trickled through Troy's veins. "What do you want?"

Bernard Beckman laughed. "That's a fine way to talk to your uncle. But then you never were one to properly respect your elders."

Troy glanced at the man waiting to take him away. "You know what I think of you." His contact's timing was impeccable. The transition wasn't coming a moment too soon. "We have nothing to talk about."

"That's just fine, Trace. You weren't the one I wanted to talk to anyway."

The dread gave way to fear. "What're you talking about?"

"You tell that woman who broke my man's nose to call her mother. I'm afraid the poor woman isn't feeling too well."

Fury erupted, chasing away all other emotion. "Don't you involve her in this," Troy threatened. "This is between you and me."

"It was," Beckman agreed. "But all that's changed now. I'm going to kill you, Trace, and this time you're going to stay dead."

Troy's bag hit the ground. "Just tell me what you want," he urged. "I'll do whatever you ask, but don't hurt that woman." He couldn't let Jane be hurt this way. Her mother was all she had.

"You give her the message, boy," Beckman warned, fury simmering in his tone. "That's all you can do. It's too late for anything else."

The connection ended.

Troy stared at the phone a moment. Then he turned back to the car where Jane waited. She hadn't left yet. She was probably waiting to see that he got on his way first.

His feet had started in that direction before his brain issued the order.

"Benson!" his contact called out. "We don't have time for this."

Jane opened the car door and got out as he neared. "What's going on?"

He thrust the phone at her. "Call your mother."

"What happened? Did Ian call?"

Troy shook his head. "Make the call."

Jane reached out, took the phone. Her hand trembled.

He hated like hell that she was being dragged into this. His heart slammed mercilessly behind his sternum. Beckman would kill Jane's mother. He had no conscience, no compassion whatsoever.

"Mom?"

Jane's face fell as she listened to the person on the other end of the line.

"What do you want?" she demanded.

Pain speared through Troy.

"If you hurt her," Jane warned, "there won't be any place on this earth that you can hide. Do you understand me, you son of a bitch?"

She closed the phone, shoved it into her pocket. "I'm going to need to keep your phone." She dropped back behind the wheel and started the engine.

Troy just caught the door before she closed it. "You need to call your agency friends for backup. You can't—"

"Get out of the way, Benson."

"Jane, listen to me. You can't do this alone. We have to—"

She shoved the gearshift into Drive and spun away from him.

"Jane! Wait!"

She roared out of the parking lot, tires squealing.

"Mr. Benson!"

Troy watched until she'd disappeared into the night.

"Mr. Benson, we must move forward with our business. We're running behind as it is."

Troy turned to the man shouting at him. The plan was already in place. In a couple of hours Troy Benson would be dead. His new identity would be born.

A fresh start, far away from here.

One step, then the next, Troy moved toward the waiting car. This was the choice he'd made. The only real choice he had.

He couldn't look back, couldn't let anything get in his way.

"You have the rest of the money?" his contact asked.

Troy nodded. "The agreement was you would receive the remainder of your money when the task was completed."

"Of course." He gestured for Troy to get into the car. "The cast is waiting to play out your final scene."

A cast of characters who would stage and act out the final scene of Troy Benson's life. A cast including the dead man.

The whole idea was surreal.

But it was the only way.

"What about your bag?"

Troy turned back and looked at the bag. Then he looked to the place where Jane had been sitting in the rental car before roaring away.

She was gone now. Gone to try and save her mother from the bastard who cared about nothing but furthering his own interests. Of getting richer, no matter the cost to others.

Troy turned back to his contact. "I need to use your phone."

"Are you out of your mind?" the man demanded. "I should have driven away when you answered a call on your cell right in front of me. For all I know," he roared, "you could have been calling the cops."

"The call wasn't about you," Troy assured him. "It was about my friend." His throat constricted as the reality of what that call meant slammed into him again. His uncle would kill Jane and her mother. "Now give me your phone." Troy held out his hand.

"Give me the rest of the money."

Troy reached for the envelope in his back pocket, passed it to the man. The bastard immediately started to count the cash.

"Your phone," Troy demanded. "It'll only take a moment."

Reluctantly, the man handed over his cell phone.

Troy slid the phone open and did the only thing he could.

The right thing.

Chapter Sixteen

12:30 a.m.

Jane parked several blocks away from her mother's home. The man who'd answered the phone had warned that if she called anyone—the police, the agency—for help her mother would die.

As much as she understood that surviving the coming confrontation without backup would likely be impossible, she couldn't risk her mother's life. So she didn't call for help. But she had a plan.

One she prayed would work.

As she approached her mother's block, she hunkered down and prepared for an ambush.

When she was a few yards from the driveway, she set her backup plan into motion.

She crouched down and surveyed the street. Lucky for her someone had already taken care of the streetlight closest to her mother's home. As she scanned the area around her, she slipped the phone from her sock and pushed the speed dial number for Ian's cell without shifting her focus from the street. She couldn't look down at the phone or whoever was watching—and they would be watching—would know what she was up to. Twisting around as far as she could while maintaining her crouched position, she left the phone facedown in the open position on the ground in the neighbor's grass.

Then she started forward once more, keeping her head low and her hand on the butt of the weapon Benson had given her.

She rounded the corner into her mother's drive. The house was dark. The driveway was empty. Her mother faithfully parked her decade-old Caddy in the garage.

Jane's pulse beat faster. Any time now—

"Throw down your weapon and get your hands up."

Jane froze.

The man who'd issued the order stepped out of the shadows. He wore black from head to toe, making him next to impossible to see in the darkness. But her eyes attuned instantly to the business end of his handgun aimed at her face.

Jane lowered her weapon to the ground. Careful

to keep her movements as slow as molasses, she raised her hands and straightened to her full height.

The hair on the back of her neck stood on end a split second before a punch landed at the small of her back. She hurtled forward. The man with the gun stepped aside. She hit the concrete next to his feet.

"Stupid bitch!"

Jane's muscles contracted with pain. She swallowed back the groans.

"Get her up," the guy with the gun ordered, "before the neighbors spot us."

The guy who'd punched her hauled her to her feet. Jane didn't resist. The pain radiating from the area of her kidneys made it difficult to breathe.

Circulation from her elbow down was cut off by his vicious grip. Oh yeah, he was mad.

Right now she didn't care about any of that. She only cared that her mother was safe. With her heart condition, suffering through this kind of ordeal…

Jane didn't even want to think about that.

The men ushered her to the back of the house. Without the streetlight or any of the exterior lights, the tree-covered yard was completely black.

He dragged her through the back door and into the mudroom.

As they moved through the kitchen, the guy in front turned on a light.

Jane blinked. The blinds on the windows in the kitchen were shut tight.

The familiar sights and smells only heightened her anxiety. This was her mother's home, the place where Jane had slept and played as a kid. No one should have to endure their home being invaded like this.

Her poor mother would be terrified.

They passed the living room and headed straight for the hall leading to the bedrooms. For privacy, of course. The bedrooms were on the end of the house where there was no close neighbor. That end of the property bordered a street corner. One of the reasons her parents had bought the property. Who would have thought at the time that same perk would be used for this?

The light in the master bedroom came on.

Jane's heart dropped to her feet.

Her mother was tied to a dining chair. Duct tape stretched across her mouth. Her eyes were wide with fear.

Jane jerked free of her captor and rushed to her mother.

"You okay?" She surveyed her mother's face as she nodded. Looked her over to ensure that there was no blood. She started to peel the tape from her mouth—

"Not so fast," one of her captors snapped. "On your feet."

Fury propelled Jane to her feet. She whirled on the two bastards waiting near the door. "Let her go," she demanded. "You have me now. There's no need to hold her anymore."

The man on the left, the one who'd punched her, then hauled her into the house, laughed. "Get another chair," he said to his pal.

The other man left the room.

If she could get close enough to the guy before his buddy returned, she could take him. She'd done it before.

"Make a move," the bastard said as he shifted the barrel of his weapon toward her mother, "and I'll shoot the old bag."

Jane's mother whimpered.

"Don't," she urged. "I'm cooperating. Don't scare her like that."

The other guy entered the room with the chair. He placed it a few feet from her mother. "Sit," he said to Jane.

She followed the order without hesitation. Doing anything to antagonize these guys would only add to her mother's fear and get her hurt. Jane understood that they knew that hurting her mother would get to her far more quickly than anything they could do to her.

The man secured her hands behind her back using the nylon cuffs. Then he stretched duct tape around her torso and the chair, securing her to the ladder-back chair. Lastly he secured her ankles to the chair legs with the same tape.

Her mother had been secured in the same manner. The duct tape wasn't a problem, but the nylon cuffs...this was bad.

He pushed to his feet and started to stretch a strip of tape over her mouth.

"Wait," she demanded. "Where is Beckman? I came like he asked, where is he?"

The guy still standing by the door laughed. "You talking about the man in charge or the fool who betrayed him?"

"I'm talking about the bastard who did this," she snarled. She hated these lowlifes. She should have killed the bastard who'd punched her when she had the chance.

"You won't be seeing Beckman." He laughed. "He's not interested in you. He wants his nephew."

A new kind of fear leached into Jane's limbs. "He's too late for that. His nephew is long gone."

"You'd better hope he's not," the man warned. "If he walks away the two of you die."

Who was this guy kidding? They would be killed anyway.

"He won't risk his freedom for me," Jane countered. "You guys have wasted your time."

The man smirked. "We'll see." He pulled something from his pocket and waved it. "Just thought you'd want to know that no one's going to be able to help you."

The cell phone she'd left in the grass. He'd found it. Ian might have gotten the call but he might not be able to track her location if the link hadn't lasted long enough.

The tape went over her mouth. Then the light went out and the door slammed behind the two thugs.

Keeping her mother alive and getting out of here was up to her alone.

Jane waited long enough for the two to move away from the door. She didn't know how much time she had, so she had to move quickly.

It was dark, but she knew her mother's room by heart. She jerked her body up and down as best she could, enough to get the chair moving toward the dresser.

Her mother started to whimper and moan. Jane stopped, tried to make a soothing sound to quiet her mother. It took a moment but her mother finally got the message and stopped making noise.

Jane scooted, hopped, trying her best to keep the noise down. Thank God for the plush carpeting.

Slowly she made her way to the dresser. Then, forcing her neck and shoulders into an awkward position, she pushed her cheek against the edge of the dresser. She scrubbed the tape's edge against the dresser ledge. Over and over she repeated the process until the edge of the tape lifted.

The slightest sound inside the house made her freeze time and again. She waited... listened... each time, then proceeded with her determined scrubbing.

By the time the tape rolled past her lips, the skin on her cheek felt raw.

She didn't bother trying to pull the tape completely free. Instead, she started the slow scooting, bouncing toward her mother.

Her heart rocketed into her throat as the chair threatened to tip over. She shifted her weight in the other direction just enough to rebalance the chair.

Then she started moving again. She reached her mother, bumped the side of her chair up to the side of her mother's while facing the other direction. She leaned to her left, and using her teeth started tearing the tape away from her mother's mouth. When her mother started to moan, she whispered, "Shh. No sounds."

When she'd gotten the tape off her mother's lips, the poor thing whimpered again.

"Shh," Jane urged. "Do you have any scissors in here anywhere?"

Her mother thought for a few seconds. "No… nothing like that."

Damn. "Think, Mom. There has to be something sharp in here."

The seconds ticked by like hours.

"Your father's pocket knife," she whispered, her voice shaky. "It's in the top drawer of the night table on his side of the bed. Where he always put it at night."

"That'll work."

Since Jane was already facing the bed, she started forward. Luckily, her father had slept on the side of the bed closest to her. She scooted, bounced her way there. She couldn't lean down far enough to pull the drawer open with her mouth.

Damn it.

She wiggled her way around, putting her back to the small table. Leaning backward as far as she dared, she finally managed to get a hold of the drawer handle with her fingers. She leaned forward, pulling it open. Leaning back again, she got her hands into the drawer, fumbled through the contents. She twisted and reached, cramping her muscles.

Finally her fingers brushed over the knife.

The first two efforts to pick up the knife failed. She had to stop a moment to relax her muscles. Finally she got a grip on the knife.

She pushed the drawer closed once more and started that bounce-scoot back to her mother. She worked for half a minute at least to get herself positioned back to back with her mom. Then another twenty or so seconds were required to get the knife open without dropping it.

"Be really still," she warned her mom. "I'll try not to cut you."

"Do what you have to do, Jane."

Jane worked the knife blade between her mother's wrists. Winced each time she poked her. Her mother never even whimpered.

Slowly, praying she wasn't cutting into skin, she worked the knife blade back and forth. Back and forth. Her heart pounded. One or both of the men could burst into the room at any second.

But she couldn't rush. Too risky.

Her mother's hands pulled free. Her gasp of relief sent the same throttling through Jane's limbs.

"Cut my hands loose," she whispered.

Her mother reached back, took the knife from Jane's fingers.

"I can't do it this way."

"It's okay. Gimme a minute." Jane scooted her way around so that she was no longer behind her mother. "That better?"

"I think so." Her mother felt for Jane's hands in the darkness. Using the fingers of one hand, she felt for the right spot, then using her other hand, she worked the knife into place and started sawing.

Jane held her breath. Listened for the approach of the men.

The nylon binding her wrists suddenly fell free. Jane rubbed her burning wrists. Thank God.

Footsteps echoed in the hall.

"Put the tape back on your mouth and hold your hands behind your back," she warned her mother as she scooted away.

The door opened and the light switched on, blaring harshly in Jane's eyes. She blinked, had just barely gotten the tape back over her own mouth.

The man stalked over to Jane and ripped the tape off her mouth. "You're going to make a statement for me."

Since she wanted him out of here as quickly as possible, she didn't argue. But she couldn't come off as too cooperative, either. "What statement?"

The man shoved a small recording device in her face. "State your name and the date. This is a report to your employer. You located Troy Benson, aka Trace Beckman. During your time with him you witnessed him murder a waitress. He used you in an effort to facilitate his escape and now he is using your mother to ensure your cooperation."

"But those are lies."

He slapped her hard. Muffled sounds of fear came from her mother.

"Fine," Jane snapped.

The man turned on the device.

"This is Jane Sutton of the Colby Agency." She gave the date. "This is my final report on the investigation of Troy Benson, aka Trace Beckman, dictated using resources entirely self-supplied. I personally witnessed Mr. Beckman murder the waitress named Patsy. He used my mother to ensure my continued cooperation. At the time of this dictation we have escaped unharmed." She glared up at the bastard standing over her.

He turned the device off with a click. "Very good, Jane. Too bad the bad guy came back *after* you'd dictated your final report. Not to worry, though, I'll make it fast when I kill you. You won't have to suffer."

He slapped the tape back over her mouth and

stalked out of the room. This time he didn't bother turning off the light, but the door slammed shut just like the last time.

She smiled, the tape wrinkling and tugging at her lips. Dumb bastard. He had no idea she'd just given the Colby Agency a message of her own. Dictated using resources entirely self-supplied stood for D-U-R-E-S-S. Duress.

The Colby Agency would know she had been forced to make the statement. However these dirtbags planned to use the statement, it was going to blow up in their faces.

She wished she could be there to see.

Moving quickly now, Jane tore the tape off her mouth and her torso. That was the great thing about duct tape, it was tough all right, nearly impossible to burst free of. Yet it tore quite easily if one's fingers were positioned on the edge and the pressure was applied in opposing directions. She used the same technique to free her ankles.

She jumped out of the chair and rushed to free her mother. They hugged. Jane thanked God that her mother was safe. She drew back, searched her mother's tear-filled eyes. "It's very important that you do exactly as I tell you. Can you do that?"

Her mother nodded.

"Chances are they've got someone outside who might spot us if we make a run for it."

That left only one option.

"You remember when I was a kid, I would sometimes hide in that place in your closet?"

"Yes," she whispered, her voice ragged and hoarse.

"That's where we're going to hide."

Her mother nodded, those tears sliding down her cheeks in tiny rivers.

Jane led her mother to the walk-in closet. She didn't want to disturb the clothes, so she crouched down and pushed aside the homemade fasteners her father had used to hold the piece of Sheetrock in place over the hole. This was actually a no-frills access door to where the small water heater was housed between the closet and the master bath. It would be cramped but they would make it work.

"Go," she said to her mother.

Her mother hesitated.

"I'll be right behind you after I've opened the window. I want them to think we sneaked out that way." Maybe an argument would break out because their man outside—and they no doubt had one— will insist he didn't see anything, but the ones inside wouldn't believe him.

Her mother crouched down and crawled her way into the cramped space. Jane put the piece of Sheetrock back in place, and secured it so it wouldn't slide out of place. Then she ensured that the shoes on the floor and the clothes hanging from the rods above were just as they had been before she'd removed the access door.

She closed the closet door, turned out the overhead light and made her way to the window. Pulling back the blind, she unlocked and raised the window sash.

Holding her breath, she dared to take a peek outside. She surveyed the side yard in both directions. Couldn't see anyone. Perfect. She counted to ten, sufficient time for her mother to have time to run across the street.

Then Jane did the thing her mother would likely not forgive her for. She let the blind bang against the window frame.

Frantic footfalls in the hall outside the door told her the men were coming. She got into position, half in and half out the window.

The door flung open and the light came on.

"Freeze or I'll shoot!"

Jane froze.

"Step away from the window."

Hands up, she did as she was told.

Strong hands grabbed her and hauled her to the

center of the room as the second guy hung his upper body out of the window to look for her mother.

"Where is your mother?"

Jane smiled. "You're too late. She got away."

The muzzle of the weapon bored into her forehead. "Where is your mother?"

"Gone." She couldn't keep the smug smile off her face.

"She's gone," the guy in the window verified. "Probably straight to the closest neighbor to call the cops."

A profusion of swear words followed, then, "We have to get out of here. Now."

And that was Jane's goal.

Chapter Seventeen

Victoria waited as the executive jet taxied along the runway beneath the bright lights. Holding on to her grandmother's hand tightly, Jamie waved wildly with her free hand.

Her mommy and daddy were on that plane.

Lucas stood on the other side of Jamie. Simon and Ian had accompanied them to the airfield as well.

There were no words for the intense relief Victoria felt. Her son was home and he was safe. Some of the burden of the past two weeks lifted from her shoulders. With Jim and Tasha here, some of the immense concern for Jamie's well-being would be lightened for Victoria. For the past two weeks she had worried that her every decision was the wrong one. For the first time in more than two decades she had second-guessed herself repeatedly.

Tasha, her husband close behind her, descended the stairs from the plane. Jamie pulled loose from Victoria and rushed to her parents. Tears welled in Victoria's eyes as she watched the emotional reunion.

Jim swept Jamie into his arms and hugged her close. Lucas ushered Victoria forward. She'd been too enthralled watching her son and his family to have the presence of mind to join the joyous reunion.

"Victoria." Jim reached out with one strong arm and hugged his mother.

It felt good to be in his arms. Tasha hugged her next while Jim and Lucas shook hands. Ian and Simon brought Jim up to speed on the events that had occurred earlier in the evening. Two men Victoria hadn't met disembarked next. Members of the elite Mission Recovery Unit.

Lucas shook hands with each and then made the introductions. "Victoria, this is Phillip Bromstad and David McCartt."

Victoria shook each man's hand. "I appreciate your support, gentlemen."

"We should get to the agency," Jim suggested, his daughter still in his arms, "so we can go over the first phase of my strategy."

"McCartt, Bromstad," Lucas addressed his specialists, "you'll ride with Michaels and Ruhl."

"This way, gentlemen." Ian led the others to the SUV.

Lucas ushered his family to the waiting limo. The driver opened the door. When they were all settled and the driver had fallen in behind the SUV, Jim turned his attention to Victoria.

"We have reason to believe Barker is in the immediate area."

Victoria's pulse skipped. "He must be preparing for the final move if he's willing to take that risk."

"That's my conclusion as well," Jim agreed. "If he's planning to make his final move, he would want to be close by to ensure that there were no mistakes."

This was a man Jim knew from his past when Leberman was in charge of his life. Barker, like Leberman, was pure evil.

"Then we don't have much time," Lucas suggested. "We'll have to move swiftly."

Fear knotted in Victoria's stomach. This was the point where anything could happen. And the risk of mistakes and surprises was far, far greater.

"Phillips, Bromstad, Simon and I will be moving in on Barker's suspected location."

Victoria exchanged a look with Lucas. "Do you

think that's wise?" She didn't have to spell out what she meant. Jim understood perfectly.

Those blue eyes, so much like his father's, zeroed in on hers. "I will see to this personally. No arguments."

Tasha looked as terrified as Victoria felt.

Jamie twirled her fingers in her mother's hair, totally unaware of the danger moving closer and closer.

Victoria summoned her courage. Jim was only doing what his father would have done were he still alive. What Lucas would do.

And if Victoria were honest with herself, she would do exactly the same thing. She had…more than twenty years ago. She'd faced whatever peril necessary. Anything to find her son.

"You're right," she said, proud of the man her son had become. "You take care of this. The rest of us will ensure that Jamie is protected."

"Don't let her out of your sight," Jim said to his wife. "Not for a moment."

Misery welled in Victoria. She'd let Jim out of her sight for just a moment all those years ago. A single moment. But it was enough time for evil to strike.

Tasha reached out and took Victoria's hand in hers. She smiled even as her lips trembled. "Victoria and I will keep her safe."

Chapter Eighteen

Navy Pier, 1:15 a.m.

How the hell long did it take to transfer a call?

Troy paced back and forth across the same stretch of concrete he'd been tracking for the past half hour. He'd gotten the number for the Colby Agency from information. Then the phone he'd borrowed from his contact had died. Since the man had already left—with Troy's money—he'd had to walk the streets until he ran into someone willing to sell his cell phone for a thousand bucks.

Now he was on hold!

He'd thought about hanging up and calling 9-1-1, but what would he say? That a woman whose name he didn't know was in danger? That her daughter, Jane—if that was her real name—Sutton, was probably on her way to wherever the trouble was going down?

"What the hell?" Troy's chest felt ready to explode with frustration.

"Ian Michaels."

About time. "This is Troy Benson." Or should he use the name from his old life? Confusion jammed his thought process. What difference did it make? "Jane's in trouble."

"What's your position?"

His position? Troy shook his head. "I don't know what you mean. She got a call—"

"Where are you, Mr. Benson?"

"The Navy Pier. You need to come now." He gave Michaels the names of the closest cross streets. "You have to hurry."

"I'm nearby. I'll be there in four minutes. Stay where you are, Mr. Benson."

The connection ended.

Where would Jane go? Her mother's home? Her home? Some other location?

If the old man wanted him, why the hell didn't he demand that Troy go with Jane?

This didn't make sense.

He turned all the way around in the empty parking lot. Standing here wasn't going to help

Jane. He needed transportation. A taxi? There had to be a taxi stand around here somewhere.

Stay where you are, Mr. Benson.

Ian Michaels had told him to stay put. Jane trusted Michaels. Troy had to calm down. He had to wait for Ian Michaels. And he had to trust him.

A black SUV wheeled into the parking area.

Troy started walking that way. Then he broke into a run. As he neared the SUV, the passenger window powered down.

"Get in, Mr. Benson."

He hesitated at the door. "Ian Michaels?"

"That's right."

Still Troy hesitated. Fear throbbed in his skull. "You have some ID?"

The man behind the wheel pulled a credentials case from his jacket and held it close enough for Troy to see.

Ian Michaels.

Troy got into the SUV.

"Where is Jane?"

"I don't know." Troy scrubbed a hand over his face. "I got a call from my uncle. He said she should call her mother. She made the call and then she got into her rental car and took off. I tried to stop her but—"

"You've received no additional calls?" Michaels increased his speed, rushing along the quiet street.

Troy shook his head. "She took my cell phone with her. I had to buy one from a kid to call you."

"I received a call from Jane about half an hour ago, but the connection was severed before I could track her position." Michaels entered a number into his cell and, to whomever he had called, said, "We have a situation."

How could he be so calm? Troy stared out the window at the passing buildings. His uncle would kill Jane if that was what it took to get to Troy. Maybe he'd do it anyway, just to make Troy pay for the trouble he'd caused.

Damn it. He should have ended this long ago.

"Have Conroy and Porter meet me at Mrs. Sutton's residence." Pause. "Yes, Jane's mother."

Troy turned to the man behind the wheel.

"No one goes in until I'm on the scene."

When he'd put his phone away, Troy said, "I can't be sure that's where she'll be."

Making a sharp left, Michaels glanced at him. "That's where we'll begin."

Too calm. The man was too damned calm. "He'll kill her," Troy felt compelled to say, just in case this guy didn't get it.

"I'm aware of the danger."

Troy tried to slow his breathing. How the hell

had he let her drive away without him? He should have done something. Anything!

"Relax, Mr. Benson, we'll be there in under ten minutes." Michaels glanced at Troy again. "If it's you your uncle wants, Jane will be safe until he achieves his ultimate goal."

Somehow that didn't make Troy feel any better. "How can you be sure?"

"There are no certainties when dealing with men like your uncle," Michaels admitted. "But that's the most probable scenario. That's the one we'll operate under."

Most probable. Great. Just great.

THE EIGHT MINUTES it took to reach Mrs. Sutton's home were the longest of Troy's life.

Michaels parked a block from the house.

"That's the rental car Jane was using." Troy's heart bumped his sternum. "She's here."

Michaels shut off the ignition. "She has definitely been here."

Damn. He was right. She could be long gone now.

With that bastard Troy had trusted for far too long.

Two other men joined them on the street. Porter and Conroy, Troy assumed.

"Head east and come around behind the house,"

Michaels instructed. "Benson and I will give you two minutes and then we're going in through the front."

The two men headed east through a side yard.

Troy wanted to run up to the house and kick the door in. He wanted to do anything but stand here.

Michaels removed a handgun from beneath his jacket. He dressed like FBI. Troy remembered then that Jane had said he was a former U.S. Marshal.

Then he made a move that surprised the hell out of Troy. He reached down, pulled a .38 from an ankle holster and passed it to Troy. He'd had a weapon but he'd left it in his bag. He hadn't been thinking. He was a research scientist. He was no good at this kind of game.

"Don't fire unless absolutely necessary and—" Michaels looked him dead in the eye "—you fully recognize that your target is the enemy."

"Got it."

"Do you have any idea how many men we'll encounter?"

"Three crashed into my house the other night. Chased us for a while." He shrugged. "There could be more."

"We'll approach from the shrubbery line that separates Mrs. Sutton's house from her neighbor. Our first goal will be to check the front windows.

Conroy and Porter will do the same in the rear. Then we'll go in through the front door."

"All right." The closest Troy had come to anything like this was running from his uncle's hired help.

So he followed Michaels's lead. When they were in position in front of the house, they separated. Troy moved to the window on the east end of the house, while Michaels took the end nearest the street corner.

The house was dark, but Troy saw no movement beyond the first two windows. The gleaming LED display, the kind found on cable boxes and DVD players, told him he was peering into the living room.

Michaels climbed the front steps, Troy followed.

Standing to one side of the door, Michaels reached out and checked to see if it was locked. The door opened. He pushed it inward.

The silence inside had the hair on Troy's arms standing on end.

What if they were too late?

Michaels went inside.

Troy moved in next.

Conroy and Porter entered through the back door.

After a quick walk through in the dark, the Colby investigators turned on the lights in one room after the other.

The place was deserted, but evidence of a struggle was in the living room as well as one of the bedrooms.

Two chairs. Torn duct tape. Nylon cuffs that had been cut.

No notes. No nothing.

Where the hell would he have taken her?

Troy picked up a piece of the duct tape.

Blood stained the sticky side.

Fear pumped through his veins.

He was vaguely aware of Michaels and the others discussing going to Jane's next, but Troy couldn't take his eyes off the blood.

If Jane had been hurt…or worse…that would be his fault. Just like Patsy's death was his fault. And maybe even his ex's.

He shouldn't have walked away four years ago. He should have stayed until someone at the bureau did the right thing.

Or he was dead for real.

"Mr. Benson."

Troy looked up, met Michaels's gaze.

"We're moving to Jane's house. If—" He stopped. Cocked his head.

What? Had he heard something?

Michaels motioned to the closet.

One of the other two, Troy couldn't remember

if it was Conroy or Porter, moved soundlessly to the closet door. A man on either side of the door, one reached out and opened it just as Michaels had done the front door.

The closet was empty.

Or appeared to be.

Michaels gave a nod and one of his colleagues eased into the closest. All three men held their weapons like the cops did when they moved in on a suspect.

The man in the closet moved the clothes on the racks aside and surveyed the wall.

A sound—maybe a whimper—echoed from somewhere inside.

Weapons leveled as a panel was removed from the rear wall of the closet.

An older woman huddled in the opening behind the wall. Troy recognized her from the photo in Jane's purse. The woman blinked. Her eyes widened as her brain registered the weapons aimed at her. She cried out.

"Mrs. Sutton, are you all right?" Michaels holstered his weapon and moved into the closet.

The woman stared at him. "Ian?"

"Yes, ma'am." He reached out his hand. "Let me help you."

When she was free of her hiding place and

assessed for injury, Troy couldn't take it anymore. "Where's Jane?"

"They took her," Mrs. Sutton cried. "She hid me in there. Made them think I'd escaped. They left with her because they were afraid I had gotten away and would call the police."

"I don't want you to worry, Mrs. Sutton," Ian said. "We're going to find Jane."

She gestured to the door. "I heard the phone ring while I was in there." She shuddered, clutched at her chest. "I couldn't make out what was said, but a message was left."

"Where is your answering machine?" Michaels asked.

"The kitchen." Her voice was weak. She'd begun to shake.

"Porter, I want you to call an ambulance for Mrs. Sutton," Ian said in that eerily calm voice. When the woman started to object, he added, "I would feel better if you were thoroughly checked out. I know how Jane worries about you."

Troy started for the kitchen. Michaels followed, calling out one last instruction for another of their colleagues, Kendra Todd, to be summoned to accompany Mrs. Sutton.

The red light on the answering machine blinked.

Troy swallowed hard, but didn't hesitate. He selected the Play Messages option.

"Jane Sutton," the male voice announced, "will be waiting at home for Trace to save her. She will be exchanged for him. If he does not come alone, she will die. If he resists, she will die. You have one hour."

The time stamp indicated the message had been left thirty minutes ago.

He turned to Michaels. "We have thirty minutes. Where does she live?"

"About fifteen minutes from here."

Chapter Nineteen

Jane Sutton's Home

Michaels broke every speed limit posted getting across town. He stopped more than a block from Jane's home.

"You go alone from here."

Troy started to get out but Michaels stopped him. "We'll get into position. I need you to buy as much time as you can."

Troy shook his head. "If you show up, he'll have her killed."

"They'll kill her anyway," Michaels argued. "He's not going to leave any loose ends. She's the only one who may have gotten close enough to prove his involvement. Or, at the very least, to verify what has taken place the past two days. We can't take that risk."

Troy hadn't trusted anyone in a long time. Four years to be exact. Jane trusted this man. He had to believe she would trust him now.

"All right."

"Hell will break loose, Benson," he warned. "When it does, it's up to you to cover Jane. You'll be closest to her."

Troy nodded.

He understood.

Her life was in his hands.

Michaels and Conroy got out of the SUV and disappeared into the darkness. Troy walked around to the driver's side and slid behind the wheel.

He drove the remaining distance to the house Michaels had described. The driveway was empty. As he pulled into the drive, he scanned the dark street. A driver likely had the getaway vehicle hidden.

Troy had a fair idea of how this would go down. When given the order, the driver would barrel up to the front of the house. Troy would be hustled into the vehicle and then they would drive away.

As long as Jane was safe, he no longer cared. This had to end.

Tonight.

He got out of the car and approached the house, the weapon at the small of his back burning his skin through his T-shirt.

His fingers itched to reach for the weapon, but he couldn't make any moves that might set off the wrong chain reaction.

On the stoop he reached for the door and it opened.

"Get inside."

He recognized the voice. One of the men who'd chased them from his house in Plano. Like before, the black ski mask prevented Troy from seeing his face.

Troy walked past the man. As soon as the door closed the weapon was snatched from his waistband by one of his pals.

"Where's Jane?" The room was only dimly lit, but she was nowhere in sight.

The man with the gun motioned to his buddy, who left the room.

"Put your hands against the wall."

Troy obeyed.

The man who appeared to be in charge patted him down.

The other man quickly returned, dragging a very uncooperative Jane.

Troy's heart squeezed. She looked okay. Mad as hell. Not that he could blame her. But okay.

Her mouth and hands were secured with tape.

"You got what you came for," Troy announced, not wanting to drag this out. "Let her go."

A gun barrel jammed under his chin. "You're not running this show. You'll follow orders or you'll both die here."

Troy raised his hands in surrender. "I got it. You're the boss." He couldn't take his eyes off Jane. He wanted this over for her.

The boss pulled out his cell and made a call. "We're ready for pickup." He closed the phone and slid it back into his pocket before turning his attention back to Troy. "This is the way our exodus is going to work."

Troy listened carefully, didn't want to make a single misstep.

"You and Sutton will go out the door first. If I see anyone else out there besides my driver, you both die. If you give us any trouble en route, she dies."

"Understood." Troy had no intention of making this complicated. His job was easy: cover Jane when Michaels and his people moved in.

The man with the gun stared at him for a long moment. Long enough for Troy to start to sweat.

He was suspicious.

"There's just one more thing," the boss said.

Troy prepared for the worst.

"You're going to change clothes with my colleague."

When Troy hesitated, as much confused as he

was reluctant to comply, the boss pointed his weapon at Jane. "Now."

Troy stripped off his T-shirt and tossed it to the other guy.

"No need to switch the pants," the boss qualified, probably because they both wore dark jeans.

The other guy pitched his black shirt and ski mask to Troy. He pulled on both.

The guy now wearing Troy's T-shirt removed the clip from his weapon and checked the chamber, then handed the impotent weapon to Troy.

"You go first," the boss ordered Troy. "Take Sutton, put the gun to her head and walk to the car waiting at the street."

Troy nodded. He hoped like hell Ian Michaels would remember his own advice: *"Don't fire unless absolutely necessary and you fully recognize that your target is the enemy."* The scumbag wearing his T-shirt hauled Jane over to him. Troy wished he could tell her that her mother was safe and that everything was going to be all right. The people she trusted were right outside. All he could do was stare into her pretty brown eyes and hope she understood that he would do his best to protect her.

When the guy motioned for him to get moving, Troy remembered what Michaels had told him. *Buy time.*

"Where is my uncle?"

"You'll know soon enough. Now—"

"No." Troy held his ground. "I want to know for sure that you're taking me to meet him."

"You do not want to tick me off," the boss warned.

Uncertainty nagged at Troy. He ignored it. "If you want me to cooperate, get him on the phone and let me talk to him. I want him to confirm what you're telling me."

The boss glared at Troy for several seconds before reacting. Then he retrieved his cell phone and put through the call.

"He wants to talk to you." The man in charge listened to whatever Troy's uncle had to say; then he handed the phone to Troy.

Troy accepted it, pressed it to his ear. "Yeah."

"Do as they tell you and your friend won't be hurt. This," he said, "is between the two of us."

"I have your word on that?" Troy almost laughed out loud at the idea that he'd asked that question. But he needed to buy all the time possible.

His uncle laughed. "Yes, Trace, you have my word. Does that make you feel better?"

"No." He closed the phone. He shouldn't have but his fury overrode his logic. He shoved the phone back at the man with the gun.

"No more stalling."

At the door, the boss gave one last instruction, "You make one wrong move and she dies first."

"I get it," Troy muttered. How many ways did he have to say it?

"Let's go."

The first step out the door was the hardest. Troy kept expecting to hear the burst of gunfire.

Jane kept the distance between them at a minimum.

She had to know he hadn't come here alone. Hell, he hadn't even known where her house was…or her mother's.

His hand shook as he held the weapon nudged against her, even though he knew it was empty.

They'd reached the halfway mark in the front yard. Sweat had broken out across Troy's brow. Where the hell was Michaels?

Jane suddenly whipped around. She knocked his feet from under him and they hit the ground together.

A weapon discharged. The bullet thudded into the ground next to her head.

Troy rolled, taking her with him.

More shots.

He had to get her to safety.

Tires squealed. The getaway car.

Troy didn't have time to see if any of the bad guys made it to the car. He had to keep Jane protected.

She tried to get on top to protect him, but he held

her down with his weight, shielded her body with his own…until the bullets stopped flying.

When he dared to raise his head, Michaels and one of his colleagues were cuffing the two men who'd come out the door with Troy and Jane.

Jane made a frustrated sound. The tape. Damn. He pulled it off her mouth. She cursed.

"Sorry."

She looked up at him, one eyebrow arched above the other. "You can get off me now."

"Oh. Yeah." He scrambled up, offered his hand and helped her to her feet. Then tore the tape loose from her wrists and removed the ski mask he'd been forced to wear.

She rubbed at her wrists. "Where's my mother?"

"One of Michaels's colleagues accompanied her to the hospital."

Jane drew in a sharp breath.

"She's fine," Troy hastened to add. "It was just a precaution."

"Thank God."

He had to smile then. "That was a hell of a good idea hiding her in the closet."

"I had to protect her."

For the first time in a long while, Troy wanted to know what it felt like to have someone care about him that much.

The sirens in the distance warned that the gunfire had awakened the neighbors and the police had been summoned.

"Jane." Ian Michaels, looking no worse for wear, joined them. "Why don't you go to the hospital to be with your mother? We can wrap things up here."

"Thanks, Ian."

When she started toward the SUV, she paused, turned back to Troy. "You want to come?"

Troy looked from her to Michaels; he gave a nod of approval. Troy hesitated before going. "Thanks," he said to Michaels. "I...appreciate all you did."

"The Colby Agency will see that Bernard Beckman is brought to justice," Michaels assured him. "No one messes with our people and gets away with it."

Troy didn't have to wonder if he could get the job done. He realized now that Jane was right, if the Colby Agency was on your case, failure was not an option.

When Troy got into the SUV, Jane was already behind the wheel. The interior light allowed him to see that his uncle's men had knocked her around some more.

He winced. "They hurt you."

She smiled, despite her split lip. "I'll live."

He stared at her the whole way to the hospital.

He couldn't help himself. Even when she shot him a questioning glance. He just wanted to look at her. She was safe. She was beautiful. And she was like no other woman he'd ever met.

Maybe he was giddy with the night's events…he couldn't explain it. But whatever it was, he didn't want it to go away.

AT THE HOSPITAL, they were directed to the fifth floor. Mrs. Sutton had been admitted for observation since her EKG showed some minor abnormalities.

The blond woman sitting at Mrs. Sutton's bedside introduced herself as Kendra Todd. She left Jane and Troy with Mrs. Sutton and went for coffee.

Troy stood back and watched the tearful reunion. When Mrs. Sutton had fallen asleep once more, Jane ushered Troy into the corridor where they could talk without disturbing the patient.

Jane had washed her face. She looked exhausted but gorgeous. He couldn't stop thinking about how beautiful she was. Mainly because he wanted desperately to kiss her again.

"I hope you'll consider changing your mind," she said, "about starting over someplace else. Ian and Simon know the right people at the bureau. People you can trust to get the job done. You could have your life back."

"You're right." He nodded. "I'm not running anymore." He brushed a wisp of hair from her cheek. "You said I was a hero." He shrugged. "Norcross seems to think I'm a hero. It's time I started acting like one when it comes to my own life."

Jane smiled, then winced.

He didn't mean to smile but couldn't help himself.

"So you'll stay?"

"Definitely until justice is served."

"What about after that?"

He caressed her cheek with the pad of his thumb. "That depends on if there's any reason to stay."

She reached up, put her arms around his neck. "Would this be a good enough reason?" She pressed her lips to his. Kissed him so sweetly…so thoroughly.

"Definitely a good reason," he whispered between kisses.

"Good," she whispered back, teasing his lips with her teeth. "Because I'd hate to have to hunt you down."

Oh yeah…he wasn't going anywhere…not without Jane.

Chapter Twenty

Thirty-six hours later

Victoria, Lucas and Tasha were standing by in the conference room at the Colby Agency. Merri and Mildred were entertaining Jamie in Victoria's office.

Six hours had passed since they had last heard from Jim and his team.

Tasha suddenly stood. "I can't stand this waiting." She walked to the window.

Lucas smiled. "You never could stand to wait."

Tasha sighed, turned back to him and Victoria. "You know me too well, Lucas."

Victoria recalled fondly that Lucas was the one to recruit Tasha. She was one of the primary reasons Jim was alive today. She'd helped save him. Had fallen in love with him even before she'd known what a good man he was beneath all the bitterness.

Victoria was very grateful to have Tasha as a daughter-in-law. She and Jim wanted to have another child. Their last attempt had ended in an unfortunate and unexpected miscarriage. The event had saddened them all. As time passed, Victoria was well aware that her son and daughter-in-law worried that there would be no more children.

Victoria hoped they would soon be blessed with a little brother or sister for Jamie.

Right now she hoped with all her heart that her son, and the others, would return safely from this mission.

And that the enemy would be thwarted once and for all.

Victoria closed her eyes. When would the past stop haunting the Colby name?

This threat to Jamie had shaken Victoria in a way nothing had since Jim's abduction. Perhaps she was getting old. Or simply tired.

The door burst open. Mildred beamed. "Jim is on the line. I've transferred the call to you."

Victoria's heart leapt.

Lucas activated the conferencing system. "Jim, is your team intact?"

"No casualties," Jim relayed, "and only one injury."

Victoria's breath trapped in her throat.

"Simon took a bullet."

"It's nothing but a flesh wound," Simon called out in the background.

"He's right," Jim confirmed. "Minor injury."

"Excellent," Victoria said, finally finding her voice.

"Are you on your way home?" Tasha asked, her face reflecting the worry that had taken its toll the past few days.

"We are en route," Jim confirmed.

"What's the status on Barker?" Lucas inquired before Victoria could.

"He and his men have been eliminated."

Though Victoria had certainly wished to wipe out the threat to her granddaughter, she couldn't help feeling regret that human lives had been lost. Even if those humans were nothing more than vicious criminals.

"I'm sure there was no way around that result," Victoria suggested. She knew her son. Though he had at one time been a ruthless assassin, that had changed. He did not take human life for any reason other than a last resort and in defense of his own life or that of another.

"That was Barker's plan," Jim said. "One of us was going to die. Lucky for me, it was him."

"We'll be waiting for you at the agency," Victoria told him.

"Well done," Lucas put in.

Tasha and Jim said their goodbyes and the call ended.

Relief, so profound that she would have swayed with it had she not been seated, washed over Victoria.

Tasha reached across the table and squeezed her hand. "Jamie's safe now. We don't have to worry anymore."

She was right. Victoria reached for Lucas's hand. "Our family is strong. We won't be outdone quite so easily."

"Hear, hear," Lucas agreed.

The courage and strength that had wavered the past two weeks filled Victoria. She wasn't old at all. And though she tired from time to time, she was far from done.

The Colby Agency had only just begun.

**We'll be spotlighting a different series
every month throughout 2009
to celebrate our 60th anniversary.**

Look for Silhouette® Nocturne™ in October!

Travel through time to experience tales
that reach the boundaries of life and death.
Bestselling authors Lindsay McKenna, Cindy
Dees, P.C. Cast and Merline Lovelace join
together in a brand-new, four-book
Time Raiders miniseries.

TIME RAIDERS

Touch Me

**by *New York Times* bestselling author
JACQUIE D'ALESSANDRO**

After spending ten years as a nobleman's mistress,
Genevieve Ralston doesn't have any illusions
about love and sex. So when a gorgeous stranger
suddenly decides to wage a sensual assault on her,
who is she to stop him? Little does she guess he'll
want more than her body….

Available October wherever books are sold.

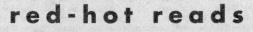

red-hot reads

www.eHarlequin.com

HB79499

REQUEST YOUR FREE BOOKS!

2 FREE NOVELS PLUS 2 FREE GIFTS!

◆ HARLEQUIN®
INTRIGUE®

Breathtaking Romantic Suspense

YES! Please send me 2 FREE Harlequin Intrigue® novels and my 2 FREE gifts (gifts are worth about $10). After receiving them, if I don't wish to receive any more books, I can return the shipping statement marked "cancel." If I don't cancel, I will receive 6 brand-new novels every month and be billed just $4.24 per book in the U.S. or $4.99 per book in Canada. That's a savings of close to 15% off the cover price! It's quite a bargain! Shipping and handling is just 50¢ per book.* I understand that accepting the 2 free books and gifts places me under no obligation to buy anything. I can always return a shipment and cancel at any time. Even if I never buy another book from Harlequin, the two free books and gifts are mine to keep forever.

182 HDN EYTR   382 HDN EYT3

Name	(PLEASE PRINT)	

Address		Apt. #

City	State/Prov.	Zip/Postal Code

Signature (if under 18, a parent or guardian must sign)

Mail to the **Harlequin Reader Service:**
IN U.S.A.: P.O. Box 1867, Buffalo, NY 14240-1867
IN CANADA: P.O. Box 609, Fort Erie, Ontario L2A 5X3

Not valid to current subscribers of Harlequin Intrigue books.

**Are you a current subscriber of Harlequin Intrigue books
and want to receive the larger-print edition?
Call 1-800-873-8635 today!**

* Terms and prices subject to change without notice. Prices do not include applicable taxes. Sales tax applicable in N.Y. Canadian residents will be charged applicable provincial taxes and GST. Offer not valid in Quebec. This offer is limited to one order per household. All orders subject to approval. Credit or debit balances in a customer's account(s) may be offset by any other outstanding balance owed by or to the customer. Please allow 4 to 6 weeks for delivery. Offer available while quantities last.

Your Privacy: Harlequin is committed to protecting your privacy. Our Privacy Policy is available online at www.eHarlequin.com or upon request from the Reader Service. From time to time we make our lists of customers available to reputable third parties who may have a product or service of interest to you. If you would prefer we not share your name and address, please check here. ☐

H109R

You're invited to join our Tell Harlequin Reader Panel!

By joining our new reader panel you will:

- Receive Harlequin® books—they are FREE and yours to keep with no obligation to purchase anything!
- Participate in fun online surveys
- Exchange opinions and ideas with women just like you
- Have a say in our new book ideas and help us publish the best in women's fiction

In addition, you will have a chance to win great prizes and receive special gifts! See Web site for details. Some conditions apply. Space is limited.

To join, visit us at
www.TellHarlequin.com.